In Memory of Onc
Tez Ya

GW00865753

CİNİUS YAYINLARI

Moda Caddesi Borucu Han No: 20 Daire: 504-505
Kadıköy 34710 İstanbul/Turkey
Tel: (216) 5505078
http://www.ciniusyayinlari.com
iletisim@ciniusyayinlari.com

Tez Yabgu
IN MEMORY OF ONCE UPON A TIME

FIRST PRINT: February, 2018

© TEZ YABGU, 2018

© CİNİUS YAYINLARI, 2018

IN MEMORY OF ONCE UPON A TIME

TEZ YABGU

Cinius Yayınları

- 1 -

"I had chosen impossible dreams; she, the freedom of fake desires."

Suddenly just one sentence started to echo in my mind. A question mark. It was sincere enough to summarize the whole subject. At least, I couldn't make any other inference after what had happened. I had long ago given up setting off on a quest for anything. It wasn't the first time it echoed and it seems far from being the last.

As the time pressed two o'clock in the night, I was driving towards Edirne[1] at a reasonable speed. A can of beer, enough cigarettes to get me through five hours and music that I wouldn't mind listening to back to back; so I had everything needed.

The night was still. Only the wind blew lightly, as if brushing off, and the moonlight was casting light on the clouds that dominated the sky in patches. My road was quite lengthy. It looked more appealing with the scenery that made my heart smile rigidly.

When the song ended and passed on to the next one, it

---

(1)   TN: Edirne is a city in Turkey, bordering Bulgaria.

was Warren Zevon's "Dead or Alive". I calmed down and cooled with an unexpected pleasure. I felt as if I owned the scene. After cursing at the darkness, sneering my lips with the attitude of winners; I took one out of the cigarette box and lit it with a swift move.

Somehow I suddenly cooled down. I realized that I was the only one disturbing the silence of the night. I took a deep puff from my cigarette and blew the smoke so that it would disperse freely in the sky. Night trips are nice. There are no people that you will have to see. Just a few vehicles passing by occasionally. Only my thoughts and I… Being alone and dancing with thoughts give me a wild joy.

My journey had no purpose. Why does there always have to be a purpose anyway? Conditioned reasonings green the seeds of hatred of the beautiful kind. The reckless waving around of a free spirit, without serving any purpose, should be appreciated. The ingenuity is in the courage of sticking by your own rules, even if you might find yourself in deep shit.

My face had become frozen whilst diving into the depths of the thoughts. I came to my senses with burning of my fingers by the cigarette, which had come to its end, burning on its own and, I realized that the song was over and the new one had begun.

With the new song, I mused in other thoughts in snatches. Each new song gestates the atmosphere of a new adventure. The sentence, defining those bleeding from the cracks of my heart, continued to echo in the pitches between intermittent thoughts. It was like a broken record, stuck playing the best part of your favourite song over and over again.

I was driving in high spirits. I didn't want the journey to end. I was leaving the concept of time to be lost, by ignoring yesterday, tomorrow, the morning and all the moments I was not present in. Embracing the night as if time had stopped, I was able to reach the deep reveries of the thoughts in the emptiness.

Some time had passed by. Maybe plenty of time had passed. I don't know. I didn't slue much attention about this. Maybe not at all... It was half past two the last time and I hadn't slued attention to where I was when I looked at the watch. None of the redundant details should occupy a place in the mind. The drudgeries of life that make you run amok, pass through being hand in glove with every unwanted thought.

Anyway. Some time had passed. I got out of the sea of thoughts and returned to reality when I noticed a hitchhiker under the lights of the entrance of one of the parking lots beside the road. Normally I wouldn't have looked and I wouldn't have cared about these. The world's human residuals are among the last things that I would slue attention to. I almost wouldn't have noticed the hitchhiker either, if the flash of the camera hadn't struck my eye from a distance. I had slowed down, thinking that it could be a radar or a police checkpoint or something like that.

When I got close enough to distinguish, I saw someone with a curious smile, holding a camera in his hand. It appeared like he had a style of his own. The presence of original people is a rare matter. I could see that the one in his hand was a professional camera. After thinking for a few seconds to take him or not, I resigned and went on without taking him. A few miles later, the sign of Kapıkule[2] appeared. I didn't look at the watch. I wasn't curious, nor did I bother. I lit another cigarette as I entered the last dark section of the road.

* * *

I had passed Kapıkule and was moving towards Plovdiv, having lost some speed. Due to the fact that I had no reason to hurry and because the roads in Bulgaria were unfavourable for high speed, I chose to go on by losing some speed. I can't stand stability for too long. Besides, I knew the road from beginning to end by heart. Watching savouringly after a long time bore a melancholic satisfaction.

At the Bulgarian side of the border, some nonconformities on my car due to some regulation changes, which I didn't really understand, were given as excuse to swindle something out of me. Although my Bulgarian was close to mediocre, it could cause problems in detailed matters. But all I knew in Bulgarian were in formal language. And when the right words are chosen towards the right person, there is no situation you can't get out of. Besides, formal language doubles the vanity.

Dawn was close. I was passing through roads that split the villages in two, moving towards the city that would deliver its own purpose. With a gloomy smile… I like

---

(2) TN: Kapıkule is the name of the border between Turkey and Bulgaria.

the way of life here. Someway people had learned how to find big happinesses in small things. Smiling wasn't expensive here. This land was a limbo-like coffin where a lost youth, who stole the future from the hands of the dead, were imprisoned inside today.

The familiar environment indicated that the distance was now quite short. The smile on my face broadened as I got nearer, and I think the longing in my heart for the scent of these moments will never cease. Nobody can take over the reins of an adventurer, who enters an unawakened city with the break of dawn to explore it once again. Especially if it is a city that depicts the very old wounds, which give pleasure when touched.

It was the eve of June, successor of the days of spring, not fully getting its share of the warmth. So it appears that the seeds of each new revolution in my life would again be fed by June suns. Once again... I can't classify it as good or bad. I just carry on my soul, the stamp of what this moment harbours. Without a hitch, every June had written different scenarios. I am moving towards Plovdiv, with nothing waiting and verging on a new June.

It was a city that stabbed hearts had deserted with tears. It was a smoky garden of tired smilets, where desires found climax, where the concept of time is totally lost. Who knows how many years, in double figures, from the end of my life was I ready to sacrifice for the last one I had spent there. Every experience in different realms of life is the adventure of a separate book. The one residing here is one of my most precious masterpieces; and again just like in the good old days, I enter this city in my favourite hours.

* * *

As the warm rays of the new day's sun that drowsed my pleasure were caressing my face, I walked towards the Maritsa River from the vacant city centre that resembled an abandoned town. It is one of my limited emotional sanctuaries, on whose shores I had made many pleasant memories dance. Besides, I could hear in my heart the reflections of the epic Balkan atmosphere and its tunes that intoxicated me as they filled into my conscious.

For a few weeks each year, transient happinesses were bought in this city. One month in every year, actual hearts were shattered. Collecting stars from the sea of thoughts while walking anywhere in it, watching the city sceneries, has become one of my most critical addictions. The ones where memories are riveted, like the Maritsa where I'm already halfway to, are at the consistency of heavy dosage. I am saving the golden shot for life's final stage.

I had reached the top of the street that lead to my favourite part of it. I lit my cigarette at a point where I calculated that its last breath would come at the Maritsa's shore, actually at a point of the street I knew very well. I could see from a distance. The Maritsa was foggy under the frost flakes of this sharp morning. Even the trees are gloomy and tending to grey. It appears that the blues will never be absent in the Maritsa's heart. No matter how much time has passed by... The scent of melancholy will be permanent on this river, for it is fed with innocent and real emotions that can't see its destiny passing into fragmentation.

As I had planned, when I reached the Maritsa's shore,

the cinder had reached the butt. In this cold morning, I started spectating with glassy looks, to the extent that my eyes could see. All thoughts suddenly zeroized. There were only raw natal gestures laden on a lifeless body, and petrifying, mournful mimics of longing.

Experiences, those on the brink of being condemned to be forgotten, those lost and found, happinesses and tears…

I heard a few series of footsteps springing in the stillness of the plain sounds of nature. So there were others who crave for watching the Maritsa at this hour, like me. Even though I paid no attention, not being detached from my usual state, the footsteps ended right beside me.

"You're late."

I answered without looking at where the voice came from.

"So are you."

It was Martin's voice. The friend by rote. One whose life is worth giving mine.

It had been a long time since we had seen each other after the great disaster. There had been no words, no news. I didn't turn to look as I answered. Neither did he while speaking. The spell would have been broken if we had looked at each other. He went on:

"I was here too long to be late. I waited here for you, on all fucking mornings of every June after you."

"How did you know I'd be here?"

"I didn't. But this is one of the places you'd visit on a June morning. Next was Asenovgrad, had you not come this morning."

"So you make a lot of miles every morning"

"Why were you so late? All times you needed to be here wasted away in a big void."

"I couldn't stay, Martin. I couldn't stay after all we went through. I needed the roads. We talked about this, though slurrily."

"You were gone in a split second. After I couldn't find you, I stopped searching and just began to wait. I knew I couldn't reach you. In fact, I started to believe you wouldn't come. You know, the dream of the North issue."

Old wounds had started bleeding again. I knew this would happen. I took two cigarettes out of my packet, lit them, and handed one to Martin. I went on talking:

"A bottomless pit formed inside of me and I jumped into it willingly. I'm still falling, going deeper and deeper. Actually there was no plan. This June I looked up again, scattered with the calling of the roads leading to the land I didn't belong to. I saw a piece of light at the top of the pit this time I looked. I think this was the sign that I'd be having a different summer. And here I am."

He turned to me and spoke in a commanding voice, holding me tight in his arms:

"Welcome to this land again, brother. There are a lot of things I've planned for your arrival for so long. Let us be merciless to the world this time. We can consider it as revenge."

We'd both cheered up and started smiling. It's a good thing to come back home and find your brother there. Together we started walking back towards the city centre. Apparently I'll be going to many places today and we'll need a car. Martin took out a flask from his pocket, took a sip, and passed it to me, thinking it would go well with the cigarette. As I took a sip, I recalled both the flask and the Old Smuggler in it. He had preserved memories well. He started smiling when he realized I'd noticed.

Walking around in the centre, Martin and I were intervally showing each other old buildings, canking of our memories and of the comments we used to make about those building since long ago. He hadn't changed. Nothing had changed. Everything was as I had left them a few years ago. Time had taken nothing, brought nothing. I loved this about Plovdiv. No matter how far away I sailed, a faithful harbour that remained the same with each meaningful stone, every time I came back...

I had left the car at the place I always did in the past. When we got close enough to see clearly, smiling again, Martin said:

"You're a creature of habit. We just can't change, can't evolve", one of the old jocular innuendoes between us.

It was a Golf 4, a relic from the old days. It was always dusty enough to take its share of grey and I never paid attention to its outer view.

"Fuck!" I said. When I saw the ticket the size of a broadsheet, stuck onto the window on the driver's side. A real torment to take it down.

"They made it paid-parking here. Back to the beginning. Same, unchanging snapshots of Plovdiv at a different time", said Martin.

While trying to take down the parking ticket, half of it got torn and stuck on the window. We jumped into the car without bothering any longer and got moving to decide our next stop that would take shape depending on our upcoming mood.

* * *

Wanting to go everywhere, we couldn't chose anywhere. That was what always happened. After driving around the city for half an hour, Martin said that he had things to do for the evening. After wanderingly taking him to his house at the South-East part of town, I moved on to pick up where I left off. As my desire of being en route to somewhere, rather than going somewhere, made itself clear, I chose not to disturb it.

A few minutes later it started to rain in medium consistency. Although it was cloudy, the rain could pleasantly embrace the smell of the city, as it cooled the hot asphalt that warmed the air.

I ended the trip, which I adorned with a half-open window and consecutive cigarettes, by passing through Ivan Vazov Street. There was a café & bar in the city centre that I'd frequented in the past, called Apartment 101.

I am planning to go underground and for this, I need to drink. When we consider past experiences, going there sober stands too high for logic to reach. Yet, I need to reach Prut. Even tomorrow is late for this. I don't need to be drunk but I must have a grasp of the situation, and having a good few drinks just enough to prevent the flurry is a convenient option. Otherwise logic absolutely objects to going there right now.

Apartment 101 is a good place for this. It has always been inspiring to me. Besides, when you spend a long time, you unavoidably gain some influence. It's not like I don't wonder if this still stands.

* * *

I was walking towards the troublesome district, trying not to care too much. When I stumbled over cobblestones a few times, I admitted that I had gone past the fair amount. I found Apartment 101 as if fresh blood had been transfused. That made me happy. The giant portraits that had replaced the artistic souvenir photos, which dominated both sides of the walls, were no better than before but this tiny detail in no way affected the atmosphere I was familiar with.

Somebody had taken my favourite corner. I was observing the interior old-style, as I enjoyed my drink. Inside, leaving myself out, were the staff, a group of girls and the ones who'd taken my place.

The ones in the group of girls were joking around with adolescent fantasies. One was a brunette, the other two auburn. They looked to be getting ready for their twenties. One of the auburns had a sweet face, while the other looked like a complete slut. The fact that the brunette was just beginning to discover herself reflected on her sweet smile, which I adored, and on her half scowled eyebrows.

As, for a moment, I thought of going over to talk to them, I turned my attention to the ones who had taken my spot. There was a nice tall girl and a guy with a hat, who looked as if I knew him from before. I could see the strong bond between them. There weren't in love or something like that but they could understand each other at a heavy dose. More than anything, I saw two long-running pals who knew the true value of the person across. To understand this is a matter that needs to be known well by looking the right way and seeing clearly. I used to have a knower like that, once. Nowadays I honour her memory.

I can say with my long-term experiences that the male was an ironsmith, no matter how irrelevant his style looked. His forearm that was bigger than his biceps and his belly below, despite his lats that made his shoulders broader, is only combined this way in ironsmiths. My long years I gave to the art of iron have proven this.

I came to the last curve before the street leading to the underground. Soon I will greet Izgrev for an unpleasant matter and my foot keeps stumbling every now and then.

* * *

A strange place Izgrev is: Gypsy district. The world changes as you enter its street. Just like the way Mexican cartels know how to enjoy life; by the way, if they were to fight in equal numbers of men, I'd bet my money on Izgrev without hesitation. It is not that they don't like strangers here, they don't care. A good side about gypsies is that, without discrimination, they give a generous place among them to the ones who can adapt to their world's jive. Also, although not recognized, they have a strong fondness to moral values.

As I expected, change happened the instant I got in. Young chaps standing in corners without any visual disjointedness from each other, with beers at hand; cheerful and amply-tattooed roughnecks getting their swerves on at raki[3] tables set in front of shops; little boys shouting behind girls in their mid-adolescent periods; a horse looking out from a window on the fourth floor; a shop-man bejewelled with golden teeth, selling live chicken next to the casino; those making out while listening to music and moving on inside a wheel-less Lada from the communist era placed on a horse-cart; and two middle-aged women arguing in heavy swear, were the first ones to strike my eyes.

The place I thought I would find Prut was three blocks away. As strangers in a hurry created suspicion around here, I was trying to walk as calmly as I could. Just as I had begun the accounting that there were three blocks after all, before I even got to the first one, a candy man stopped me to ask, as part of his job. I slid around in a way that wouldn't cause trouble.

I had arrived at the last block without problems. I turned with a reflex when someone behind me called out. The previous dope dealer appeared with a hooker whose breasts were just maturing. The girl tried to sell herself too with a smile. As I turned this down too, two other guys appeared behind me. Looks were frozen and you could cut the atmosphere with a knife. The bossy one of the two behind me started talking, keeping his cool:

"You don't want dope or women. So what are you doing here?"

Although I couldn't see the right hand of the guy behind him, I had recognized the sound of the opening snap blade knife. If I made the right moves, I could knock

(3)   TM: Rakı is an anise flavoured alcoholic beverage specific to Turkey; similar to the Greek Ouzo, and Arabic Arak, but is less sweet.

down the two who had appeared and break the candy man-pimp combination guy's neck. However, even if the problem is a small one, a troublemaking stranger cannot get out of Izgrev so easily. It was best to openly tell them my intention. And besides, back in the day, Prut was among the limited number of people who could frack prostitutes free of charge.

"I came to find Prut"

The snap knife was put back and the bossy one suddenly became friendly. Curving his lips, he said:

"Brat? Why didn't you just say you know people from the inside? You'll get yourself killed. Whatever, take care."

As they walked away as if nothing happened, the pimpy candy man turned and said:

"If you can find Prut, tell him: No more broads for free."

At least this time around wasn't so difficult. I remember clearly the troubles of one of my visits here. I had come to a Turkish-speaking barber at noon time. Just as I was almost there, a man, who got out into a balcony in the next door building with a pump-rifle, had shot at another man sitting at the coffee shop across the street. Nobody had died because the buckshot spread at a distance but I was rewarded with the duty of eye-witness that had ruined my whole day.

As they moved away, music from the shop around the side came to my ears. There were again drinking roughnecks but they had an extra luxury compared to the previous ones: One of them was playing rock classics on an accordion. Of course since he only knew some part of the riff by hearsay, he could just hum along randomly. I had finished my last cigarette as I enjoyed "Another Brick in the Wall" and "Paranoid" in turn.

When I reached the street I wanted, I entered the small grocer at the corner and bought a box of Davidoffs. When I got out, a half-naked guy sitting at the stairs of the house across the street was giving me the stink-eye while smoking his cigarette. He had blonde wavy hair that stuck out of his black Stetson, and a tattoo, that went from his innie to his throat, of a crucifix above the clouds with transparent angel wings. He was thin but his arms looked big and strong for his body.

I lit a cigarette too and started plodding along towards him. He got up in a very calm way and began stretching with his hands clamped behind his neck. I hadn't gotten halfway when someone past by me running with a club in his hand and headed across the street. He was running with fury to attack the stretching man but when he got close enough, the man suddenly stopped stretching and bent slightly forward, he spit the cigarette in his mouth towards the guy with the club, and caught and twisted his wrist. With a move I couldn't quite see, he bent his arm backwards and leaned on the twisted arm of the guy with both hands. As ear-ripping cries smeared in a clump sound of breaking, I got a little nauseous, also with the effect of alcohol, when I saw the broken bone come out a few inches after tearing the skin. He had leaned on the arm at an ill angle. He had already strangled and put the guy out before I reached him. After I puffed out the deep breath I took from my cigarette, I looked at the fainted guy on the ground and asked:

"What was your beef with this guy?"

"I had given his sister moments that she couldn't forget. Apparently he couldn't stomach it."

"You're a total psychopath. You know that, right?"

"I get nice complements from a professional sociopath. You're back. Did you come to Izgrev to collect your debt from me?"

"Maybe. Would you like me to?"

"I don't think so. I like owing you my life, Attila."

"For now I just came to see if I could find you, Prut. But I didn't want to find you this way, just as I had left you."

"What did you expect me to do?"

I took the flask out of my back pocket, took a sweet sip, and passed it to him:

"Remember your dreams. The ones you put aside on dusty shelves… Remember your impossible dreams!"

He pulled a long face. After he took a long sip from the flask, he suddenly growled with anger and tossed the flask far away, and he walked away, huffing and puffing. I had now wakened the one who needed to wake. I hailed a cab on the street and left Izgrev, with the intention of coming back.

* * *

Darkness had fell by the time I reached Martin's house. I had encountered an unexpected crowd as I got in. Martin didn't used to be an actively socializing guy and the inside was no different than a hencoop.

"Where did you get so many chicks?" I asked.

"The trio in the lounge jumped in as soon as I opened

the door", he said smirking "Lee brought them. He is in the room I spared for you with two other women."

"Whoever this jerk you call Lee is, it seems we'll get along well."

"I'll introduce you when he gets out. He is one of the types the soulless society hasn't blunted."

He put a glass in my hand and went into the living room, tilting his head sideways as if asking me to follow. He sat across the two dames inside, clinked drinks and turned to me:

"Let me introduce you. The one on the right is Petya and the one on the left... Sorry I can't remember because it was an uncommon name", he said in English, "by the way, where is your third?"

She turned her looks at me with sharp nobility and with a tone that wriggled me inside, she stabbed a name that came from her small pink lips into my ears:

"Evdokiya. My name is Evdokiya."

She had blonde hair, which gold would have a jealousy attack over because of being pale beside them; and blue eyes, which would make the liveliest skies hide behind dark clouds with shame. With grace appropriate for a lady, I held the hand that she held out to shake hands.

"приятно познакомиться. меня зовут Attila. рад вас видеть!⁴" I said. All my language tabs were mixed up. She was the first person to make me feel like this after a long time. She was one hell of a woman.

With a smile that became her lips "большое спасибо⁵",

---

(4)   TN: Russian for "Nice to meet you. My name is Attila. It's a pleasure to meet you".

(5)   TN: Russian for "Thank you very much".

she said, "Your friend didn't realize I'm Russian. That's why he was a stranger to my name."

"Possible. By the way, it was a nice gesture for you to turn back to English. My Russian sucks. I'd like to understand you fully."

Repeating the same smile, she said, "I noticed. You have a funny but cute accent. It's obvious that you're not used to my language."

As if thanking, I first hit her glass and then the others' and took a double sip. As per my advice, we were talking only about our plans for this week when Lee came in with the dames.

Slapping Martin's shoulder, "Oh! The massage was so good, bil", he said.

"Did you just massage each other?"

"Of course just massage. Did you think we were prostitutes?" said one of the girls as she pushed Martin's head aside.

"I don't keep pissy-arsed company, bil", added Lee.

"Look Lee, this is Attila. The only guy I call my brother."

He was smiling interestingly as we shook hands with sincere firmness. He was weird. I think in time, all disturbed people develop the skill of noticing one another at first glance. I warmed to him quickly. Considering that I couldn't stand the majority of people, this was not a small deal.

It was obvious from the first moments that Lee was out of standard; with his frequent interesting smile that striked the eye; with his quick comprehension of women, although he looked like a pervert from a distance and his speaking out with both sides of his mouth; and with the way he didn't smoke with alcohol and went through the night with chocolate and fruit milk although he had a spark in his ass like a cokehead.

The evening was passing with quality spraff that I enjoyed plenty. I was sure I would find new things of my liking when I came to this city, whereas I am quite distanced and prejudiced for novelty. I had begun finding them just at the bosom of the first moonlight.

As much as I could make out from their talk, Lee was old friends with Evdokiya's older sister and Evdokiya had come to Plovdiv as an art editor. It was chosen as the capital of culture or art or something this year. I wouldn't have noticed if she hadn't said so. I already forgot which one it was.

As for the other two girls, we're all seeing them for the first time. They met Lee on their way to Bulgaria last night. They were the dullest of the group. I dwelled on them no longer.

In the moments I could take my attention off of Evdokiya, the most striking one was Lee. I couldn't even realise when Martin and Petya disappeared. The third girl of the trio was still nowhere to be seen. Actually, I had seen her only vaguely at the beginning.

Lee had a very familiar complexion. As if we had recently dealt with each other. I was surprised when he said his age was over 30. One of those who looked far younger. Probably because he insisted on always staying positive. He was a photographer too. That was even weirder.

"Well… So you met on the road yesterday. I arrived

yesterday too. It appears we missed each other", I said, to rake it up a little.

"We almost missed each other too, if Lee hadn't used the flash in the middle of the night", said the girl who was drowsier.

I silently hurled a swear of surprise. Now I remembered him. He was the hitchhiker with the flash. I put a bold face on. Leaving them in the laughter of the changed topic, I went out to the balcony to smoke.

The rain had just began drizzling when I got out onto the balcony. The temperature was close to making you sweat, despite the rain. It was as if the lustful sounds of raindrops making love with the leaves was heating the air. Raindrops were hitting with rut and the leaves moaning insatiably.

It was just the rain to feed iron. Instead of quenching, while I forged the frameworks of my statues, I with used to fill the hot iron with raindrops. The raindrops needed to fall like a legendary poem that made the soul dance, like an unforgettable melody.

By the way, it had been a day where the rain hadn't taken a rest. Wow! Even the month of June was weeping in the mourning of my return. The sweetness of the days I missed was in the air. My drink was finished. I had to get one from inside but I couldn't leave the taste of the moment halfway.

I lit a cigarette. My eye kept slipping towards the Pole Star that challenged the Moon. Suddenly the balcony door opened and Evdokiya came in, or rather, came out with two glasses of wine in her hands. Damn! She had chosen wine for me when there was a big bottle of whiskey in there. But I felt a bittersweet joy, thinking of what wine conceived.

The sound of Tom Waits' song "Yesterday is here" came from inside. She handed the glass to me and took a long sip, looking into my eyes without saying anything. It was as if the glass surrendered to her lips' drunkenness, melted with deep pleasure while contracting with shyness.

Again saying nothing, she held out her hand towards my face, with a slow and gentle manner as if trying not to scare a timid butterfly. She slid her hand over my cheek, skimming me inside, and took the cigarette in my mouth and brought it between her lips that made the glass tremble. She took a gentle drag and:

"I thought maybe I could make you talk in the dark of the night", she said. Her eyes were almost dancing before the moonlight.

"What can you expect to hear from a man who has nothing to say?"

"You are truly a closed book. The chat that went on for hours contained no traces of yesterday or no expectations of tomorrow. Just the things brought by the time in it, and out-of-vogue ideas…"

"Aren't these quite enough? Besides my yesterday and my tomorrow are things that keep averting each other. Nothing interesting."

"I still think I can find a way to hear these."

Still looking into my eyes, she twisted her wrist and emptied the wine down the balcony, and sent the empty glass after it. Two of her fingers had gotten wet as she emptied the glass. She held out her hand slowly once more and spread the wetness of the wine onto my lips. She pinched her eyes, which she had filled with moonlight, and leaned towards me, taking my lower lip between her two lips.

The heat of the night turned into a hallucinogenic drug and began to blur all the facts outside the focus of passion. It was as if raindrops murmured the melody of passions, evaporating halfway and raining again and again with the desire to stop time and immortalize the melody in the universe.

Her lips met the moist of wine and roamed on my lips as if following a roadmap. She drew back to let the moonlight out from her eyes, where she had imprisoned it.

"I want to see your statues. Maybe I can start there. Art is a manifestation", she said, winking her mesmerising eyes.

We set on towards my house in Asenovgrad, which had turned into the tomb of my dusty statues. Ahead, we had a half-hour of road and the melody of raindrops engraving into the depths of the universe.

- 2 -

I tiredly opened my eyes. I tried to apply the tactics I used to have for understanding what time it was. When I half-opened the curtain and looked outside, it was sunny and the shadow of the tree in the yard had passed the corner of the wall. So it was about 2pm.

I got up from bed and put something on. The Blues songs of the seventies echoed inside. As I got into the kitchen Evdokiya was mixing something inside the pitcher, while rocking her head to the rhythm of the music. She only had my favourite black jacket on. When she saw me, she smiled in way that lightened up the day and said:

"Доброе утро[6]. I made orange juice for you. It will help you recover", and she finished her glass in one gulp after handing me mine.

A sharp burning skinned my throat as soon as I sloshed the glass with thirst. She had just given colour to a brimful of vodka with orange.

---

(6)   TN: Russian for "Good morning"

"I didn't know they made orange-coloured vodka", I said, half smirking.

She chuckled too, showing her teeth, looking into my grimace.

"Давай, мой герой[7]. The coming days will be long", she said and added, "I will meet a successful painter named Valeria at the culture house today. They say she is a bit arrogant but she is also said to have a beauty so influential that it overshadows her paintings", as she winked and went into the room to get ready.

When the morning vodka made me feel good, I began to grant her right. I lit a cigarette and looked onto the street out of the window. Old days appeared before my eyes again. The roads that were wet with last night's rain had begun drying in patches with the new day's sun. The pavement stones were again frayed, the trees leading down the street again pollarded, and Mete Aga's, who sweltered due to alcohol, window again ajar. His turn in my list of visits was coming up. Suddenly the sound of the phone broke the silence.

"Hello!"

"Hello, Attila. It's me, Martin."

"I was just coming over to you. I haven't stored your phone number."

"Again? Anyway, listen to me. I just talked to Seven. Prut is out of Izgrev and he called Seven to a name duel."

"Name duel? I guess this guy wants to get into alcoholic coma."

---

(7)   TN: Russian for "Come on, my hero".

"What alcohol coma? I said he is out of Izgrev. I wonder how that happened."

"We'll find out. Anyway, I'll see you at Place of Seven Sins then"

"No wait. First I have business with Lee in the centre. Lee doesn't know them, I better not get him in there. Let's meet at Apartment 101."

"OK. I'll see you."

"See ya."

As I pulled Prut's pin, things became to develop curiously. Nobody had taken down Seven in a name duel before. That's why we still call him Seven!

Seven was a clever and wise guy. He liked comprehending and ceremonising critical events. In the past, if someone had a problem he couldn't solve, he would consult Seven. And he, without exception, would find a way of solving everything. He was sort of a modern age philosopher that didn't go amiss. He never engaged in anything but drew into initiation time to time.

He had rented the first floor of an apartment building in the centre and turned it into his private bar; only after cherry-picking did he accept a few people in there. All the upholstery was distressed wood. He had a couch that he let nobody touch, and only that couch was outside the wooden decoration. He never sold anything for money. As a matter of fact, the ones who came to drink brought their own drinks. Seven's wave was solid. That's why he called it Place of Seven Sins. Hence the nickname Seven. To learn his real name, you need to beat him in a name duel. So far, except for the one person that beat him, he has told his real name to nobody. Actually, the guy whom he did tell is no longer alive.

Suddenly I had mental pictures of my unforgettable memories at Place of Seven Sins. Anyone who has blended in those memories can ever forget that place. It was the roof under which we spent the most time, having the time of our lives.

After the great disaster, the great abandonment, no one of the main community was there anymore. Everyone scattered like a defeated army, shouldering their own pains. Just like I did… In fact I was surprised at Seven still being here, as much as I was at Martin.

With the arrival of Evdokiya, I realized that I had to get ready too.

After dropping Evdokiya at the culture house, I moved on to Apartment 101. It was empty but for one person. I had beat Martin and Lee to it. While inside, I was both surprised and also a bit angry. The male one of those who had taken my place last time around was here again, and again he had taken my seat. I was sure he was aware of the taste of the place he got.

He was writing feverishly on the piece of paper in front of him, one which he hovered over; then he would suddenly stop for a few minutes, stare out of the window, and go on writing again. He was almost not aware of what was happening around him, he didn't want to be.

Just out of curiosity, I purposely sat a few tables away from him. His movements were influencing. While with him, the whole world could feel alienated against his inner world. Maybe he really had excluded the entire world. Who knew…?

I went out to the balcony to smoke. Apartment 101 had two storeys and a balcony with a nice view that overlooked the post office and central park. The sun not only brightened the greens of the park, but also honoured, with nostalgia, the big post office that defied years. A view that looked like it sprang out of a postcard would find life in Apartment 101's window, not only in the sun but also in snow and rain, in any kind of weather.

"I had chosen impossible dreams; she, the freedom of fake desires", I hummed to myself and the thoughts of the memories that I had buried in the deep prepared their whip. Admitting that there is no way away from this, no matter how much I run, I am waiting in the pitches of this life to bear all that I deserve.

With the hatted man who took my place coming out into the balcony to smoke, I suddenly found a way out of the thoughts I avoided, even if temporarily.

Although he stood right beside me, he was again moving as if he saw no one, as if he was alone in the whole world. Rhythmically he was taking a sip from his coffee, a drag from his cigarette, consecutively and in turns. He was looking neither at the post office, nor the park. He was watching the in-between, almost trying to look at the furthest point possible. He quickly went in as soon as he finished his cigarette. Just then I caught a glimpse of Martin and Lee, who were coming from the side of the post office that lead to the centre.

After taking some beverages, they both came to where I was. Martin asked:

"Did you wait long?"

"As much as I needed. What did you do?"

"Nothing, shopping. Lee bought those shinny shoes. He really likes shiny stuff, like a disco ball", he said, showing the contents of the bag.

"I needed shoes, bil", added Lee, showing his ever-interesting smile.

"Your needs never end anyway."

We were talking about such superficial things, dwelling on the issues at length. I was waiting for Evdokiya. But there was still plenty of time. Besides, we couldn't miss the great duel at Place of Seven Sins beforehand. Talking about relationships again, as the subject branched out, Martin asked:

"Lee, aren't you getting married yet, by the way?"

"How can I get married? Is there someone to marry? Where are they?"

"What do you mean there aren't any?

"There aren't. I can't find one."

"OK man, then tell me! But be honest. How many girls have you had till now?"

"OK man, I'll be honest! I stopped counting after 500."

"Yet you still say there aren't any girls."

"I say there aren't any girls to marry."

"What's the difference? What do you expect?"

"She should never have kissed before, bil. At the same time, she should be smart and belong only to me. And she shouldn't smoke, that's enough I guess."

I intervened, "OK Lee, was there ever one out this more than 500 ones that you couldn't forget?"

"Of course there was. There is one that I don't forget even one minute with her. But let's talk about this some other time", he said and got up to go to the bathroom, again with the same smile.

"Interesting guy. No matter how much shit he falls into, he never gives up on his smile", said Martin, looking into my eyes as if waiting for me to ascribe a meaning to this.

"The deepest wounds are compensated with the most false smiles", I said, taking basis my own life, which I filled with many examples of it.

We both shut up. Martin understood very well what I meant. We didn't need many words in our communication with each other. So much time had passed but we still hadn't sat privately to talk properly. And now we were silent.

When we look at each other, we can see on our faces the scars that the events we lived through left on our souls. Maybe that was why we didn't need spend too many words. For us, how the other was effected was more important than what we lived. The lost looks of an exhausted man in me, dim smiles tired of longing in him... Two brothers, watching each other's remains.

With creaking of the door, Lee came back to us, and Martin and I once again assumed the false smiles, which we began to be fond of. An offer came from Lee, who was known to be fond of table games:

"C'mon let's go play pool. We can play three-ball."

* * *

After we left the pool place, Lee left us saying that he would visit someone he knew at the Medicine College.

And we headed towards Place of Seven Sins. It was already close to where we were.

We were there in a quarter-hour. The door opened as soon as we rang and Seven stood before us with all his grandeur. He was tall and strong. He was one of the, so to say, numbered survivors of the great disaster.

He was a dignified man and he watched me without breaking his stance, as if he was not at all surprised. Then he hugged me like a warrior would. Only after that could he smile. Afterwards he started to laugh out loud. There, that was it, the reaction of the accumulations of an old friend.

"Oh boy! Ha ha... So you're back, huh? Come right in", he roared, laughing loudly.

He immediately made us sit on his famous couch and took two bottles from the bar and put them in front of us along with two glasses. The bottle he put in front of me was a half-full Old Smuggler. It was quite a dusty bottle. As I dusted it off, Seven chimed in:

"That half bottle is the one you left here on your last night", he said.

"And you kept it all this time?

"Of course. So that you'd surely come back and drink it one day."

"So you were expecting me to come back?

After saying "Of course you would. Everyone returns one day. That's why I keep everyone's last bottle. So they may drink it on their return", he turned his head towards the bottle placed at the top of the bar and murmured silently "At least for the ones who can return".

It was a half-full bottle of Flirt at least as dusty as mine. Zed's bottle.

"He was a man of honour", I said.

We just kept silent. Clinked our glasses and afterwards I got up and went to the bottle. It wasn't just dusty. It had dried soil stains on it too. And a few strings of grass, glued on it with the drying soil. When this raked my memory a little bit, I remembered. I remembered crystal clear, at that.

Zed had had his last drink with me. We were on the balcony at the 13th floor and he was telling me the decision making of the event that took him away. And I had got mad at this decision and tossed the bottle from the 13th floor down to the empty land on the side. I couldn't change his mind no matter what I said.

Seven's habit of knowing all but saying none. So the bottle hadn't broken, actually Flint bottles are really strong, and he found it and kept it.

"Attila! Come sit, let's chat", Seven called out, "so? Was Vitebsk nice?"

"Vitebsk? Where's that?" Martin jumped in.

"The place Attila went. A town in Belarus", replied Seven immediately.

"How come? How do you know? Or rather, what didn't you tell me? Or were you in touch from the start?"

"No. I just know. I know everybody's. Don't ask too much. I know because I don't tell."

I was even more surprised. I had just taken off and nobody knew. Nobody.

"In fact it was quite clear he was going north but there

are thousands of towns. I was very surprised you knew directly", grumbled Martin, scratching his head.

* * *

We were lost in conversation. What we talked and did were like an ordinary day that was torn from the past. We were getting angry at and laughing at the same things. We were almost talking in whispers in the room calmed by the music.

Suddenly there was a knocking at the door with the sound of two strong and clumpy fists. The whole room was covered with silence instantly. It was two fists that were cool enough to win the approval of even the angel of death.

Seven rose up slowly and lumbered along to open the door. A while later, first Seven and then Prut, as drunk as a sow, came in. He had a serious face. After greeting each of us, he took a sip from the first bottle he got hold of, and turned to Seven.

"Are you ready?" he asked.

"I never needed to get prepared. However, you don't look so ready."

"I just warmed up. We'll see in a while who is ready."

They were standing across each other like two gunfighters waiting for the clock tower to toll, talking without moving their bodies.

"Let me remind you of the rules", said Seven. "Whoever passes out loses. You will drink it one gulp no matter the size of the glass, and you lose if you throw up. Plain and simple."

"Is that all?"

"Also you choose the type of drink and the size of the glasses, I choose the music. That's all."

"Let's not belabour then. My practice is dropping", said Prut and went behind the bar, dragging his feet.

First he took a look at the bottles on the top shelf. Turning up his nose as if showing his dissatisfaction, he eyed the bar end to end. Then he smirked like he had done some bravura and leaned under the bar. Following some bottle rattling, Prut came up with three bottles of tequila in his hands.

After he put the bottles on the table, he went back to the bar to choose glasses. This time he had much more options. As he took them all one by one in his hand, trying to study them, Seven was digging into his record archive on the other side. Setting his eyes on a wine glass he held in one hand, he was weighing the Turkish tea glass with the other. Suddenly the wine glass in his hand cracked. With a loud voice, as if scolding, Seven said:

"Choose the thickest glass. I don't want to be left without glasses later. You've started breaking them already."

After looking at glasses some more, Prut came back with two small rakı glasses. They weren't too big but if they were to toss it down, they needed at least three gulps.

The table was arranged, glasses filled, music set and Seven started ceremonizing:

"Sky in, red out.[8]

If I fall, the name you get.

---

(8)   TN: An important oath for the ancient Turkish. Sky symbolizes steel (sword) and red represents (blood). Roughly means: "If I don't keep my word, a sword should be thrust and my blood should be spilled".

If I rise, glory and fame is mine", he said and in the honour of the take-off, he sent contents of the duel glass, which he prepared by mixing every drink he had in the bar, down the hatch. He never changed his habits. He was one of those who lived life like this, from the beginning.

The first drinks were poured. They both drank at the same time. Immediately the next ones were poured and they went on like this for a few more rounds. Smiling, Seven said:

"I hadn't been challenged for quite some time. It felt good after a long while. I won't hurry to add another notch to my victories."

"Then you've never competed a Gagauz before", replied Prut, as he took the next glass to his mouth.

The next few rounds also went by joyfully. After the ninth round, they slowed down the tempo a bit. They were making small insinuations between rounds. Prut had already arrived drunk. Seven was no less than him. As rounds went by, they both started turning red. Prut was really into it, as if winning was his greatest goal, like he had to.

Time was flowing and the intervals between rounds getting longer. They had passed 20 a few rounds back. Prut's eyes began to redden and squint. Seven remained composed from the outside but his voice became empathic, his movements got slower.

Prut became really serious. Seven looked more like he was concentrating. Prut was clenching the table with his empty hand on one side. They had really lost the thread of the quantity.

After drinking two more rounds, Prut almost fainted.

Although he looked as if he was trying to hold onto life between his eyelids, the seriousness in his face kept growing.

Drinks were filled one apiece. Seven could drink only by completely contracting himself. Prut, at first, could barely hold the glass. Then while he was drinking, he began coughing before he could make the second gulp and half of the glass was spilled on the floor. Smiling, Seven said:

"That's tough!"

Prut had put his head on the table, trying to breathe deeply. He lifted his head up slightly, looked at the table, and gazed at it for a few minutes. His lips curled, his red eyes got even redder and a teardrop from his tear trough slid off his nose. He closed both eyes and grimaced even more.

All of a sudden, he slapped the table with all his might and with a voice born of a deep pain:

"For Zed", he shouted and stood up, grasping the half-empty bottle and finished it with a series of gulps.

He rose at full speed like a jet trying to go over the clouds and stopped just as he reached the clouds. His hand holding the bottle fell to his side. The bottle slipped from his hand, clanged as it bounced a few times. First his head fell and then he collapsed as his knees uncoiled.

We were all covered in silence and wondering what would happen now. It had created a small shocking effect.

Seven got up calmly, filled his duel glass and went to the bar, clinked it with the dusty Flirt bottle at the top. Then he slowly went over to Prut and whispered into his ears a name that we did not hear.

* * *

I was going towards the culture house. A hot day had passed and now the warmth of the evening started spreading around. I had left Martin behind to sober up the dudes. The limits of alcohol had been overly exceeded, refrained words spent more than necessary.

Yes, Zed. A lost life, a man of honour, a valiant who made no compromises from his pride and a dearly missed brother... The only brother we lost on the one road of no return.

We went back a long way. Our brotherhood feelings were kneaded with a rooted bond. We shared almost every existing emotion that we went through. We told each other everything, we shared the feeling created by the experiences. We had heart-to-heart talks when we were sad, drank together with joy when we were happy.

Sometimes a man wants to tell his secrets, which he had hidden in the darkest corners and which he can't even remember on his own, to someone whom he trusts more than himself; but there is never such a person. Well, there was for us once. Maybe we had become so close because we could comprehend each other's points of view perfectly.

Everything started one day with his telling of his penitent secret that would initiate his journey of no return. Actually it wasn't such a complicated matter. In fact, it was a shackle in its simplest form, one that had dealt with a majority of people.

One day he had called me to his apartment on the 13th floor, or I had went there myself, I don't remember exactly. He had painted all the walls of apartment blue and he was drunk as a skunk. This wasn't a small deal because he was the only one who could learn Seven's name. I realised then, that somethings would go awry.

He was trying to speak but words kept sticking in his throat. I could see that he was struggling under a very heavy influence. Even his gaze, due to shame or helplessness, could not keep still. I wanted to tear out the venom inside of him with my claws but I didn't even know what it was.

When he gathered himself a little bit, he told the matter with a few words. He had fallen in love with a Persian girl with dark blue eyes, called Lammim. It seems the solution to this simple yet mighty issue will never be found. Time will pass again and this international intoxication will crush many brave ones inside its palms.

Zed had fallen into the desire of possessing a forbidden one who belonged to someone else. Maybe they could band together as one in another universe but there was no room for miracles in this reality we are stuck in.

Knowing this quite well, Zed had surrendered himself to the wind, which dubiously blew about with desperation. And most, he was burning inside because of not being able to defeat desperation. He had painted the walls blue in her honour, accepted leaving his liver behind, for starters.

His passion had flared up in time. A giant ball of fire that grew with time and burned away every beholding eye…

There, after this time everything changed step by step. This ball of fire gave birth to and began to feed an ever-growing fury. It was such a strong curse, one that stained another underserving.

After a while, he began to look for ways to spill out his anger and found himself in cage fights. This is the time when Prut joined us. Prut was an immigrant, one we had no idea where he came from. One of the limited number of things we found out about his past was that he had received a tough training by the last Sayokan master in Komrat, that he rose to the level of mastership and that he had taken the habit of getting into cage fights for fun. He had respected him after Zed beat him honourably and in time they had started fighting together.

I had watched every stage of the change in Zed. He was losing all his goals in life one by one, increasing the number of fights and drinks day by day. He was so lost inside his pain that sometimes he forgot why he was fighting, and he fought only for the hell of it.

I tried to talk him out of it on the night before his last fight. I had tossed his bottle that night when I couldn't succeed. He didn't listen to me and the next day he got into his last fight where I would personally witness his death.

He and Prut were a team. It was a tough fight. Our guys were giving the others a good tonking at the start. While Prut was wrestling the big one, Zed had already taken the other one under him and with his fists, he had brought him to the point of passing out. But Prut stopped on a dime and held his left chest.

We would much later learn that Prut had a hole in his heart. The hulky one, taking advantage of Prut's hesitation, had stunned Prut for a few seconds with a fist he landed on his jaw. These few seconds destroyed a few lives.

The hulky one then ran to Zed and before Zed could realise the situation, he jumped and leaned against Zed's nape with both feet. With a "snap" sound that trembled the whole world, boiling waters turned into a flood that would last forever.

After that day, the first stone slipped and signs of the great disaster began to occur one after another. The hulky guy suddenly vanished into thin air. Prut never forgave himself and locked himself in Izgrev, leaving everything.

I was behind the wheel and my bones started shaking as I thought of all this. Inside, I could feel the presence of a volcano that was losing its astuteness. I felt the pressure inside my eyes. Not now. Boiling tears couldn't drop. I was going to meet Evdokiya soon and watch the mirages of happiness again.

I felt stiffened. I lit a cigarette to cool down and just as I thought I had settled down; I hit the steering wheel, yelling from the top of my lungs, "I lost the person I cared for the most because of the things brought by a silly love rout".

The horn honked and a silence spread as if I had brought my fist onto the street. The cars next to me had slowed down. As if all the attention was gathered on me. "Whatever!" I said, not caring much for the crowd. Anyway, you can't tell to those who have only heard of heaven, about an angel raped in hell. Right?

* * *

When I reached the culture house, Evdokiya wasn't waiting for me alone. She was with an auburn dame, where sexual elements had peaked. As I stopped by the pavement where she was waiting, she opened the door and bending down, she blew me a kiss and asked:

"Would you accept a guest for a dinner out?"

After I nodded yes, they both got into the back seat. They must have had a nice day because they were never out of smiles. Evdokiya reached out her hand and as she rubbed my chest over my left shoulder she said:

"Let me introduce you. This is the painter I told you about; Valeria. When we couldn't go through everything we wanted to talk about, we said why not end it at dinner?"

"Nice to meet you ma'am", I said, looking at her face in the rear view mirror. It was as if her eyes had turned hazel, just to match her brown hair.

"Same here. Actually, I was quite curious about you after what Evdokiya told me."

I looked once more from the rear view mirror. Evdokiya was right. She was very beautiful. A dangerous beauty. So dangerous that it could raze every weak one to the ground, even make many of the strongest ones' lives miserable… Anyone who can, should stay away.

It would be rude manners not to join into the ladies' choice. We passed on to a Chinese restaurant close to the culture house. The food was nice and we chose an appropriate local Mavrud wine.

As the conversation got deeper, the pace of the wine also began to accelerate. It was like Valeria was loosening up a bit and Evdokiya was getting a little nervous. I think

Evdokiya was beginning to see the reality that I saw from the beginning. As she drank, Valeria was gearing up her loose manners, sometimes getting close to the point of provocation.

At one time Evdokiya got up to go to the bathroom and the two of us were alone. After one, one-and-a-half minute, Valeria sighed and said:

"So I hear you have fascinating statues. I want to see them the first chance I get."

"Too late. I don't take part in exhibitions anymore."

She asked "so what? Your statues didn't just disappear, right?" a question that she already knew the answer to and added, "Besides, if I can see your statues at your house on my own, I can feel them better", winking prominently.

She inhaled deeply, further featuring her already big breasts and curled her lips slightly, bringing them close to a kiss. But there was one thing she couldn't realise. The more erotic she became, the cheaper she seemed in my eyes. I guess she was comparing me with the men she twisted around her little finger. Probably because of the ego of having anything she wanted, any time she wanted.

Her ego must have blinded her so much that she didn't realise that I cared more for the quality of the soul before the quality of the body of the one standing across me. Shame! She is pathetic for me and she doesn't even know this.

She was very beautiful, though. If she hadn't had too much wine to loosen up too much and picked the right words, she could have probably added me among her victims. But the curtain had fell and the medallion had flipped to the other side.

When I returned with a slight smile, I guess she was surprised at not getting what she wanted and got a little furious.

Complaining, "So you don't really want to show them?" she bit the right side of her lower lip with the tip of her teeth.

As I felt a heeled shoe against my foot, Evdokiya came back and the heeled shoe withdraw in a flash.

"No mischievousness, right?" asked Evdokiya jokingly, smiling meaningfully.

Obviously Valeria was a professional at what she did. She didn't have the slightest evidence in the actions.

"If you had been a little more late, we would be bored stiff", she said with a smile that made her look oblivious to everything.

"It's getting late. Let's get going, if you like", said Evdokiya.

After the closing acts, we dropped Valeria at her place and headed for Asenovgrad. The nervousness on Evdokiya's face hadn't quite gone. Silence was trying to get it out of her chest. When she noticed it too, she said:

"She looks like a very dangerous girl", seeking approval.

"I'd seen more dangerous ones. Ones whose presence only bears the danger of perishment…"

"How destructive can a danger that you know of be?"

"That's probably what they said while eating the forbidden apple."

"Then this means wanting the one to be stayed away from, venturing bearing the consequences."

"Yes. But wanting is one thing, doing another."

"So what are we doing? Where are we moving to individually?"

"This is a question that I quit searching the answer of, a long time ago."

"Then tell me. Who made you quit searching?"

"Just as the owners die when their names are remembered for the last time, I buried that name into the day I last remembered it."

"Блядь!⁹" I had left a bottle on the back seat when we left the house", she said. Turning, she reached for the back seat. Her thighs were right next to my face. She looked like she was trying to seduce me. After she found the bottle, she drew back, rubbing her thighs against my shoulder. That really worked.

After taking a sip from the bottle she handed it over to me, asking "Want some"?

My hand slipped for a minute but then I gave up. I realized once more that I was fooling myself. Despite what I had said, maybe even inside every unit of pieces that fit into the concept of time, I recalled her name inwardly. I lit a cigarette and took a very small sip from the bottle she still kept up.

"It's like you are living a spiritual masochism. If you would talk, you would break the chains, but it is as if you can't give up the pleasure of keeping silent…" she said as she took another sip from the bottle.

---

(9)   TN: Russian for "Damn!"

"Whatever. There is a long night ahead. By the way, see how beautifully the moonlight flickers", she added, on our way to Asenovgrad.

* * *

It was past 5:30 a.m., before 6:00 a.m. I was out of smokes and I had to go down four blocks to the market working 24/7. A distance one wouldn't want to walk at this hour and at this exhaustion rate. Still, I gathered my strength and set off.

Suddenly a cat jumped out from Mete Aga's garden. Then another one... When I got curios and went in to look, I saw that he was arranging a place for himself to sit in the arbour.

He was a man with some blood in his alcohol. Someone who was in a different dimension than the society he was in, thus not understood.

He constantly got drunk three times a day then sobered up again. Apparently I had caught him in his first start in the morning. I went up to him like on an average day and called out:

"Good morning, Mete Aga!"

"Oh! Welcome Attila. When did you get back?"

An old dog, Mete Aga was. He had gone through times I wished I had seen.

"Not long ago, Mete Aga. Let's meet afterwards if you have the time."

"Suuure! Knock my door at noon," he said, that being his second shift of drinking.

After nattering for a few more minutes on our feet, I

was back to getting cigarettes. Thankfully, I must be lucky, the market at the corner was opening up. This saved me from the walk I dreaded.

* * *

A short while after noontime, I knocked on Mete Aga's door. He lived on the ground floor. I couldn't make myself heard the first time. When I tapped on his window he gave out a sound and went outside in slow motion.

"Mete Aga, come be my guest."

"Do you have any of my medicine?"

"You bet!"

"Wait then. I'll grab my cigarettes and come."

When he went inside to get his smokes, I too, lit a cigarette as I waited. Right then, a woman sitting on a short wall down the street caught my eye. She was embracing herself, swinging slowly. I couldn't really make it out from a distance but it was as if her lips were moving. I guess she was talking to herself.

"Who's that woman, Mete Aga?" I asked out of curiosity after Mete Aga came out.

"She was a fine woman. Her pain is rather big. I'll tell you inside."

Since our houses were right across each other, we got into mine in a few steps. Evdokiya was still sleeping in the room next door.

I took glasses, an ashtray and a bottle of good quality bourbon for Mete Aga from the kitchen and went into the living room. Mete Aga was looking a bit puzzled and a little curious. I had arranged the glasses neatly and had just started pouring when he asked:

"What's this?"

"Your medicine, Mete Aga. The best bourbon whiskey I've got."

"Oh Attila! Don't you have domashna rakia?"[10]

"No. What do you need that for? This is much better."

"Nope. Take that British piss away."

"OK, Mete Aga. Then wait and I'll get one from the corner" I said and headed out for the market at the corner.

As I approached the market, I was also getting closer to the woman I'd seen before. She was shaking as I had last seen her and indeed talking to herself. This was the inability to stand a heavy load, rather than common insanity. The tears that dropped from the sides of her eyes once in a while proved this.

When I got back, I saw Mete Aga as I had left him. I quickly changed his drink with the one he was expecting and sat next to him.

"Well, Mete Aga... Tell me now. Long time no see. What going on?"

"Let me not leave you hanging, Attila. It has been three years since I got out from this neighbourhood to the centre. You were here, no?"

"Yes. It hasn't been that long since I left."

"Really, you remember, right? That time it seemed to me that the centre had changed a lot. I'm enjoying myself here. I don't care about anything else."

---

(10) TN: A Bulgarian home-made rakı, mostly made by Bulgarian and Turks.

"I noticed, Mete Aga. And you haven't eased up on the booze either."

"Suuure!"

"Fine but, Mete Aga, you haven't taken care of yourself ever since I've known you."

"I've got domashna rakia! That's my medicine. It doesn't any let any germs or anything live on."

"At this rate, it'll probably not let you live on either."

"Look, Attila. I had a close friend once. No smoke, no booze… He used to collect herbs from the mountain over the Balkan to live healthy. He passed away at 40. Look I'm still standing."

It was an answer that raised question marks. He could have died of several reasons. I wanted to rake it up a bit, also so that Mete Aga would sober up.

"Fine, that maybe true but, Mete Aga, what did the man die of?"

He hesitated for a moment. After thinking for a while, scratching his white beard, where the moustache part had turned yellow because of smoking, as he said:

"Now, Attila. The guy is dead. You can't ask him how he died", without bearing any joke, fully seriously, I couldn't help but laugh out loud.

After listening some more from Mete Aga about the news that had happened during my absence, we eased down a bit. Taking advantage of this I asked Mete Aga:

"You were going to tell me about the woman sitting on the wall down the street, Mete Aga."

"She is a woman who suffered a lot. Fill this glass so I'll tell you."

I filled the glass in front of him. Lighting a cigarette,

he leaned back and finished his glass thirstily. He reached for the bottle himself and poured twice more than I had into his glass. He fanned his cigarette and:

"She had a beautiful child around seven-eight years old. She suffered a lot for her child, that woman. She gave up all her youth. So that her home was a happy one. But the kid was very sensitive and withdrawn. So sensitive that he couldn't stomach some of the jokes. One time when their relatives were at home, they teased the boy jokingly. How could they know that the kid would resent it so much and take it as a matter of pride. Suddenly the boy started shouting and ran to the roof. They couldn't even hold him. Then the woman after him…" he said, taking a strong gulp from his drink and went on:

"The woman begged but she couldn't make him stop, Attila. The kid let himself into the void. Poor woman. How could she know this would happen? She lost everything. Herself too… So, even if for a child, there is no border for pride. The most devastating bombs make explode in the tiniest of hearts.

I paused for a moment. Even if I knew nothing about the woman, it was heavy. I shivered a little when I put myself in her shoes. It's not easy, especially if it is a mistake of someone with such a good heart…

Sometimes the things that pure hearts knead with great effort, could come down with a small bit of negligence, in this motherfucker life. So every flower that blooms in this swamp should be preserved with care.

We said nothing for a few minutes. Mete Aga took another sip from his drink and said:

"They showed the Cyprus landing on the Turkish

channel today, Attila. I remember those times. I was in my twenties too."

He lit another one as soon as his cigarette was finished. His voice cracked and his eyes become redder than the reddening of alcohol. His eyes were full. He was crying inside. Obviously his face was tired but his insides, the inside of his eyes were crying. His eyes were so full, even if tears didn't come down. With his trembling voice he said:

"I couldn't go, Attila. All my agemates in Turkey went. The communists didn't let me. I couldn't pass the border and join the Cyprus landing." He was very full. He didn't stop:

"I wanted it more than anything. They held me at the border, didn't let me go."

His face was red, hands starting to shake. I was seeing Mete Aga like this for the first time. I wasn't expecting something like this at all. So no matter for how long we know someone, we can't truly recognize him.

Just as he was settling down a bit, he winced at the sound of the bathroom door. Probably Evdokiya was awake. We couldn't see the bathroom door.

"Oh! Was there someone in the house?" he asked.

"It's OK, Mete Aga. A friend of mine is staying over."

"I'll leave then. I don't want to bother you."

"It's no problem. Stay some more."

"It's fine, you get comfy now. I'll see you again."

"OK, Mete Aga. Let's meet again", I said and after sending him off, I went in and knocked on the bathroom door.

* * *

We were out for dinner in Asenovgrad. Evdokiya was wearing a black and elegant dress. How many more times did she want to impress me?

We had sat down and relaxed. She was watching me. She was doing the same thing again. Again she was filling the moonlight into her eyes.

"I need to tell you something", she said. As she breathed, minutes became longer, the moonlight became even brighter.

"You don't have to say anything, if there is an upcoming trip."

"There will be a largely diversified international exhibition in London next week. I have to attend, as part of my job. After that I'll return to Moscow."

"So this is our last week."

"We are the destitutes of adventure of the wrong time", she said and then winking with a bitter smile, she added "If everything had gone well, it wouldn't have fit our lifestyles anyway."

"We are just the right people slightly touching the right place at the wrong time", I said.

"I wish…" she left it halfway. When she couldn't rule over her voice, I went on:

"Who knows, maybe we'll meet again while fiddling with the pages of a much different and far away life."

"There'll be an extensive section for statues at the exhibition in London. I know it's asking for the impossible but maybe you'd want to take part."

"The thing to convince me has to be really strong. Besides, I'll never take the old ones out of their place."

"So when was the last time you made a statue? Maybe it's time to make a new one."

"I don't know. I hadn't thought about this for so long."

"Shall we go? Let's walk along the creek a while."

We got out of the restaurant and started strolling along the creek. She ran into a nearby shop when she saw it. A few minutes later she came out with a bottle of local Mavrud wine.

"I liked this a lot. I liken it to you."

"Interesting", I said.

While walking along the creek, we saw a nice bench and sat on it. We had to break the top of the bottle because there was no corkscrew.

As if what we talked about at the restaurant was never mentioned, we were having a casual night. At one time the bottle's broken neck cut my lips. Evdokiya slowly touched it with her finger and said:

"My favourite part of your lip is cut. Let's go home so I'll take care of this. Besides there is an issue I'm curious about."

When I squinted my eyes as if asking with curiosity, a few words that shook the night spilled from her mouth:

"Am I strong enough to persuade you? That's what I wonder."

Her sweet smiles were challenging another star.

* * *

I slowly opened my bleary eyes. The first lights of the new day shone on my feet, coming out from the gaps between the curtains. The room was cool and I had a sweet tiredness although I hadn't gotten out of bed for almost two days. My skin was as if smoothened. As I straightened up in bed, Evdokiya came into the room with two coffee cups in her hands. God, this chick keeps bringing me things to drink.

She was just out of the shower. Her hair was wet and wavy. Her eyes shone even brighter upon meeting the light of the new day. She was keeping the front of her bathrobe open. Wetness had embraced her body and a few drops of water slid down over her breasts as she walked towards me. She was a masterpiece, crafted with as much attention as a fiery angel's portrait. One of the masterpieces of God's unique art…

Maybe what fascinated me the most was her physical resemblance to Miranda. And her choosing the right words at me, like her.

"Every day we spend together, we add a new page, which will remain unfilled, to the end of the book, don't we?" she said and she sat next to me, starting to massage me with her hand.

She scraped my skin with her bare body, leaned over towards my lips and started kissing me somewhat roughly. The daylight was stretching out down her thighs, as if making the moonlight jealous. We were honouring the daylight with the fiery angel by gathering multi-coloured flowers from the gardens of sin.

She determined the rhythm of my heart with the warmness of breath. As she was on top of me, she spread her arms fully and leaned backwards. Even the angels with the most majestic wings couldn't dare challenge this. Her voice echoed and walked on the daylight, and our souls were once more excommunicated from innocence with the last sound.

She held me across my waist, leaning her head on my left chest, and with a thank you kiss, she made the hours of the new day start working again. She reached at the coffee cup on my other side, took a sip and lit cigarettes for the both of us.

"Come with me to London. I want to display your statues in the exhibition. What was the name of your awarded piece?" she said, blowing the smoke onto my chest.

Once I had received an award with a statue that whipped my inner conflicts with slander. It was an obscene statue of a woman smiling with teardrops. The statues left hand was on her belly and the right hand was crossed over onto her heart.

"The Goddess of Whores" I replied. "The Goddess of Whores in Remorse…"

- 3 -

Evdokiya had bought two tickets for the plane to London, leaving from Plovdiv airport two days later. I would be back soon but Evdokiya's destination was very different and probably we were having the last of our time together.

I wanted to go through this day without alcohol. After wandering around in the park for a while, I went to Apartment 101 since it was already quite close. And for the sake of having a healthy day, I was inclined towards a double espresso and fresh orange juice.

Well! Lucky at last. As I went up the stairs of Apartment 101, the man with the hat, who had always taken my seat till now, was coming down. I could finally sit in my favourite place.

The stairway was narrow and we both had broad shoulders. He was just a little stockier. We could pass only by the both of us turning sideways. He was obviously disturbed and he passed by me with an ill-humour.

Lee called as soon as I sat at my favourite table.

"What's up, my man?"

"Fine, Lee. Trying to wake up. How 'bout you?"

"Nothing. We were gonna go out with Martin but he ditched me for a girl, asshole."

"I'm at Apartment 101. Come by if you're close"

"Great. I'll be there soon. You get things ready."

"C'mon, I'm waiting. Grab a packet of Davidoffs on your way, will you?"

"Got it. See ya."

"See ya."

I had ordered the things I had in mind while waiting for Lee to come. A brunette chick with the left side of her hair cut flat did the serving.

Apartment 101 really livened up in the next 20 minutes. The orange juice and espresso livened me up too. I felt quite hearty and fresh. There was nothing bothering my mind since the morning and I was in a good mood. As I thought Lee was just round the corner, the phone rang again.

"Attila! You naughty bastard. You came to Bulgaria and you don't call me, huh?"

"I haven't been to Sofia yet. I was going to call you when I did, Albena."

"You never used to call unless you needed my help in the old times too."

"I'm a guy who calls when he feels like it. You know that."

"C'mon, get over with it. Didn't you miss me at all?"

"Missing is relativised with deprival, rather than time."

"So your absence has been very destitute."

"My whole existence is full of deprivation"

"Come as soon as you can. I'll give you the best. As always…"

"Be careful, the boundaries of daringness is a fragile one. Besides, don't forget, I've always hated my weaknesses trying to cuff me."

"It's that protest attitude of yours that turns me on the most. Don't forget to come to Sofia. I've still got the same address."

"All things apart, I enjoy your convo the most, you know."

"And my throat…?"

"I beg your pardon?"

"I mean I doubt that my only feature you like is my chit-chat."

"Give the devil her due! I'll look for an opportunity to come but it's not a promise."

"We'll see. Let's talk again later. Bye for now."

"OK. Bye."

Lee stepped inside as I was putting down the phone. He looked tactless and carefree as ever.

"Hey, Attila. What're we gonna do man?" he grumbled without losing his cheer.

"What do you mean, Lee?"

"You know. Even Martin stood me up."

"Why?"

"Why? For a dame of course. Everyone gets a lover."

"Why don't you get one, too?"

"C'mon. You know why."

"What about that dame you can't forget?"

"What about her."

"Go after her."

"It's too late now. There are long years and a couple of thousand miles in between."

"Lee, why don't you just tell this thing straight?"

"Come, let's get outta here. The weather's fine. I'll tell you in the park. And, we can check out some chicks."

"OK", I said and got up to pay the bill.

* * *

It was chirpy as a cricket when we got out to the park. Lee got even more cheerful. Why had I asked about the guy's wound and undermined his buzz?

The park was full of model-turned-mothers walking around with their babies. Most of them were looking at Lee with the corner of their eyes and Lee was quite aware of this.

"Dude, what kind of mothers are these? Did these kids come out from these?"

"Maybe they're aunts, Lee."

"No, no. These are mums. Anyway, that bench over there has a nice view. Let's squat there."

We beat an adolescent group to it and got the place. Lee rubbed his hands together and clapped, asking:

"So, my man. Which part do you wanna hear?"

"I don't know. We've got time, Lee. Tell it all the way. Like, what was her name?"

"Her name is Alina."

"How did you meet?"

"It was about six or seven years ago. I was in Antalya for the catalogue shoots of a modelling agency. I was waiting at the hotel lobby when she came to the hotel with her family. I was entranced as she walked to the reception with that fascinating air of hers. She had a snow-white dress on her. Blue eyes looking through her black hair… It was like her dress was the clouds. Her eyes were the sea, her hair the dark night and her wheat-skin the endless beach…"

"So you were lucky. Everything went exactly as you could want."

"Easy, huh? The girl was just 17 then. Besides, she was completely preserving herself. She stood by me with such nobility that her eyes wouldn't glance anywhere, even slightly. Just the girl to make her man proud! It was very difficult for me to approach her."

"So… What was so difficult about it?"

"Like I said, she was under-aged and very conservative. And her father was a merchant. At that time I was at my shabbiest. Also I was in my youth, when I was living it up to the fullest. In one week I got a reputation in the hotel as a playboy. The toughest part was breaking this prejudice."

"But you got her in the end"

"Yeah! Tough as it was… We had had a great month. That was the last time I was truly happy. We were living as ready to let everything go. Before her, even the woman in my dreams couldn't be so perfect."

"If the issue was so deep, how did separation fall in?"

"The holidays were over and she had to go back."

"Is that it? So simple?"

"No, of course not. We never lost contact after she left. I looked for ways to go to her for three years. All that time she patiently waited and kept calling me insistently."

"What was holding you back?"

"Money! Actually, lack thereof. I had messed up big time in the stock market before that. As I tried to regain my loss at gambling tables, it became doubled. It took a long time for me to get my act together. Now I'm an expert on gambling and I'm flying high in the stock market, but she's not there."

"As hard as it was, you could have gone to her and try to pull through there."

"If it were you, would you make a loved one suffer while you couldn't even support yourself?"

"You're right. So how did you end everything after waiting for three years?"

Lee had got serious. He was serious for the first time since we met. So were his tone and his voice. The smiling mask he had imprisoned himself in was gone, his scabby wound was swollen. He took a sip from the bottle of water in his hand and answered my question:

"After waiting for so long, she had to move on with her life somehow. She called again one day. She said she didn't want to cheat on me in any way but she had to go on with her life. She asked for the last time if I would come and I couldn't be selfish any longer. I guess there no evil more merciless than giving people false hope and stealing their years for nothing. What if had told her to wait and never get there?"

He took another sip from his water. And I lit a cigarette. He tried to cool his pain with sips and I tried to blur the sharp reality with a few smokes.

"And everything was over with that, huh?" I said.

"Not exactly. For about a year, we kept on talking every now and then. We felt good to hear that the both of us were getting better. I gathered myself up and she was together with someone who would make her happy. In the end she said that she got engaged and that it wouldn't be appropriate for us to talk any more. After that we never heard from each other."

Good hopes and a bad ending... Lee put his mask back on. Smiling, he said:

"Let's go out tonight, my man. Maybe I'll find a new match. Tell the guys to join us."

"Got it, Lee. I'll go get Evdokiya then. I'll also call Martin and tell him to let everyone know. Tell me when you decide where you wanna go. We'll meet there."

* * *

Evdokiya had to prepare for the night so we went home early on. Actually I hate loud places other than concerts, and night clubs, in addition to this, also have those wannabe dancers. Still, as I had no plans for the night, I found it suitable to blend in with my company.

Lee has chosen a famous night club by the Maritsa River. It didn't amuse me at all, and I had let Evdokiya decide on what I was to wear.

We were to meet in front of the place, as decided. We saw a huge crowd when we arrived there. Everyone who was at Martin's place on the night we met with Evdokiya was there. We could hardly find the others among the crowd.

When suddenly the crowd became too suffocating,

Evdokiya asked to leave even before we got in. I felt suffocated too and acknowledged her to be right.

When I said "We came all this way. Let's at least have a quick drink and then leave. For fuel…" she agreed. The place hadn't really striked Martin's fancy either. We were like a bunch of troubled sociopaths.

According to one of the girls who joined us said, a popular singer would be there. That was why the place was stowed out. As we got inside, the other girl with us said that we had a reserved table. They had turned the bar in the middle of the place into a stage and our table was a few rows back, across the left side of the bar.

Before Evdokiya and I knew it, orders were taken. A bottle of vodka for the girls and a half-litres of milk for Lee…

Lee's milk was fine but what the hell was vodka for! I'd rather drink metho. I added triple bourbon for me and Evdokiya. We were going to stay only for one drink anyway. I didn't plan on making that miserable.

Some of the people were trying some nonsense dances to the music played before the singer, and Evdokiya and I had to shout into each other's ear to talk. People talk about socializing here but they can't even talk and hear what is said. A tormenting contradiction!

We had finished our glasses before the singer even got on stage. After arguing with Martin, we decided to leave after the first song. Martin would join us with his new girlfriend beside him.

After waiting a little while, a woman with a bad accent and moves like a street corner prostitute came onto the stage. We had already gotten our coats and reached the exit door before the first minute of her song.

* * *

We were at Martin's place and chilling again. The girls were renewing the snacks as per their own tastes, and Martin and I were doing nothing further than hitting the glasses one after another. After first wearing off Martin's broad Psychedelic Rock archive, later we were reducing time into the small pieces of sand inside an hourglass, making them fall one by one, with the alternative Russian songs Evdokiya chose.

Everyone had their favourite drinks and enough smokes to make them be consumed faster. We were as if in a spiritual massage, like the pleasure of meditation. We were spread out onto the sofas and couches with both mental and physical relaxation.

"So you're kidnapping Attila to London, huh?" Martin complained jokingly to Evdokiya.

Evdokiya went along, saying "If I was skilled enough to kidnap him completely, we would be having our breakfast in Moscow the other week".

"Take it easy. He just got here. I'm not letting him go anywhere."

"Don't get me angry. I'll use all my trump cards if necessary but I'll somehow lure him to Moscow. Then you'll be chasing after tickets to Moscow", she said to Martin smiling friendly. Then she laid her head on my shoulder and turned her eyes up, to me and said:

"You haven't seen my ace in the hole yet, мой герой"

"I raise the bet even against the best trump cards of my opponent, just for the hell of it, моя звёздочка[11]."

Patya kissed Martin's neck and turned to us, saying. "I see you got used to each other more quickly than it could be imagined".

"And look who's talking" added Evdokiya and they both burst into laughs. Martin and I had also laughed, but at very different things…

While Evdokiya was under my arm, I gave Martin the fig sign with my hand around her shoulder and said in Turkish "So you hear, the sounds we like finally echo inside the house."

Petya threw one of the lighters on the table at me and said "Hey! Speak Bulgarian or English so we can understand you two perverts. Even Russian is fine but forget the other languages".

She was right. It was an inappropriate thing for a gentleman. I straightened, buttoned up and smiling ashamedly, I said in Bulgarian:

"I'm sorry ma'am. You're right. To make amends for myself, I will read you the only Bulgarian poem I know". Then I coughed intentionally and started the poem:

Жив е той, жив е!
Там на Балкана,
потънал в кърви
лежи и пъшка.[12]

---

(11)   TN: Russian for "My star"
(12)   TN: "He is alive, alive! There in the Balkan, sinking in blood, lying on the ground" in Bulgarian.

Petya was surprised but she liked it all the same. "Pretty irrelevant but I liked this." she said.

Evdokiya poked me in the belly, saying "I'm waiting for the same performance in Russian".

I smiled and kissed her forehead after I hit my glass against hers. I knew I was headed for drunkenness. I was completely in high spirits. A beautiful day was ending and I was letting my face tingle a little with the influence of alcohol. God, sometimes it can be really easy to smell happiness.

* * *

We had spent the night at Martin's house. My side was empty when I woke up. The mattress was garbled and a torn bra was hanging over the pillow. As I tried to get up, I felt a series of burnings in my upper back. When I turned myself sideways and looked at the bed, I saw small drops of blood at my side.

I got up and went to the cheval glass. What I saw when I tried to look at my back were large and small, swollen and reddened lines. Claw marks…

When I got in, at first I couldn't see anyone. Only after moving further and hearing the girls' laughter from the balcony, could I realise that they were sitting there. The door of Martin's room was open and he still hadn't waken up. First I disturbed Martin enough to wake him up and then went to the kitchen to make myself some coffee. After that I went onto the balcony, where the girls were.

"Good morning girls!"

"Good morning!" said both.

While standing, I got a cigarette from the table and after taking a few puffs, I let myself down hard onto the empty chair next to Evdokiya. I rose up as soon as I leaned my back. As I felt dozens of needles sticking into my back, Evdokiya looked at me and giggled, asking:

"What's wrong? A prick in your back?"

When I looked at her, I saw the rash on her necks. Hers' were obvious marks of sucking.

"I guess a bug bit me at night. A female tarantula, I reckon. You know, the one who eats her man after having sex", I replied.

"You're confused. That's black widow", she said, kissing my neck.

A few minutes later Martin came holding his head with ache, eyes hardly open. He, too, lit a cigarette and leaned on the balcony rails when he couldn't see an empty chair.

"I have a splitting headache. How much did we drink last night?" he said.

Petya got up and made Martin sit on her chair, then she sat on his lap and answered:

"Too much for you to remember certain things."

"I need to get home to prepare for tomorrow's trip", I said to Evdokiya.

"I'll come with you. All my stuff is there anyway", said she.

"Fine. But I'll visit Atanas and Teodora before that. Friends of the family… Then I'll come and get you."

"Forget those nut-heads. One time, everyone was walking around high because of them", interrupted Martin.

"Really, we've got a trip tomorrow. Can't you make your visit after you get back? We have only limited days left together", added Evdokiya.

She was right. I was going to be back in a week or two anyway and as far as I could guess, I would be spending much more time here.

"Very well. Then let's get to Asenovgrad now. It may take some time to gather the tools I use in making statues. I don't even remember where half of them are", I said.

* * *

By the time we reached Asenovgrad, the midday sun had started slapping the earth. The sun, was making Asenova Krepost shine, as if manifesting itself as God's gift.

Asenova Krepost was the name of a castle that harboured a very old church. It was build right under the entrance of the mountain range. It stood with all its majesty as the ancient guardian of Asenovgrad, carrying the old generation's memories for the next.

When we got home, the door opened as Evdokiya turned the handle.

"Блядь! Did you forget to lock the door?" she asked a bit nervously.

"Maybe. Don't worry, no burglar will come in here. At most, it was Mete Aga, coming in and out with hope of finding raki."

"Who's he?"

"Never mind. Short story but don't bother."

"Whatever. We don't have anything else to do but get ready, right? I'm asking because I'll prepare a drink that will lighten up the getting-ready part."

"The kitchen is all yours", I said and kissed her neck, hugging and smelling her.

It was time for me to get ready for a passion of mine, which I hadn't practiced for a long time. My hands were covered in cobwebs in that regard. I was a ruin of an artist and I still couldn't find the strength to lift the debris off of myself.

Most probably I wouldn't be able to build anything successful but I have to tauntingly obstinate with life to make it even angrier. Life feeds on the ones who are aware from the beginning that they will lose against it, and this makes it even more merciless.

Maybe the path to victory against is lies in embarking, enjoyingly and without hesitation, on battles that you know you will lose before they start. Just for the hell of it.

Evdokiya served the drink she had prepared, again turned on her favourite Blues songs, put on something cosy, and started packing up while swinging with the music.

After I finished the first glass with a smoke, I took a sip from the second one and left it on the coat stand in the hallway, and went out into the garden.

In the garden there was a hut, previously a coal-shed, where I stuffed the gadgetry. I went in head on and started to toss out every tool that could be useful. I could find only some of the necessary tools but it wasn't a problem.

I was mainly trying to reach my sledgehammer at the deep end. I couldn't forge iron without it.

After scratching around for quite a while, I reached its handle. When I pulled, like the roots of an uprooted tree bursting the soil, it came into daylight scattering everything.

It was an heirloom, 33-pound handmade sledgehammer. At the time, my father had given life to the shamanic motifs on it, engraved them with care; and he had written, in Gokturk[13] alphabet, the aphorisms from my oldest known grandfather to the current one.

My real name wasn't Attila. I had gotten this name according to old tradition. I was only ten years-old and when I took the hammer in my hand for the first time, and hit the hot iron for the first time, I had felt a deep sensation, a spirit entering me and the iron surrendering against it. My father, who said he saw these in my eyes, said "From now on you are Attila[14]. May his might always be with you" and gave me this sledgehammer, his sledgehammer.

The one and the most blessed heritage I had was this sledgehammer. I could feel that I engraved another oath onto the iron with my every strike. One day, when I stood before my ancestors in the Tian Shan[15] I would be able to prove my loyalty to them, with my head held high.

---

(13)   TN: The Göktürks (Celestial Turks, Blue Turks or Kok Turks) were a nomadic confederation of Turkic peoples in medieval Inner Asia.

(14)   TN: Attila, frequently referred to as Attila the Hun, was one of the most feared enemies of the Western and Eastern Roman Empires, during his reign of the Huns from 434 until his death in March 453.

(15)   TN: The name "Mountain of Gods" was given by the Turks, who accept it as their first motherland.

I remember that day explicitly and as I held the sledge-hammer in my hand, it became entirely clear. I could feel the vibration of the blood in me. Time stopped. The wind stopped.

Out of my will, adrenalin rushed to my hand holding the hammer. One of my spirit lightnings around my eye flashed and, turning into a thunderbolt, it striked my wrist. With all my strength, I swung the hammer from under, in the shape of a crescent, and the hut's door exploded like a cannonball.

Oh God, was it happening again? I can't remember exactly. Was it because of this that I hadn't held this hammer for so long?

My eyes settled down as Evdokiya got out.

"What's going on?" she asked in panic.

For a moment I didn't know what to say. First I looked at the shattered door and then to Evdokiya… What could she understand, had I told her?

"Nothing. I was checking if I was rusty", I said.

"What sort of check is this? You outright scared me."

"You're the one who wanted me to build statues. Think of this as the opening. Consider it an artist's vagary" I said, smiling so as not to frighten her any more.

"You're crazy. That's why I want you so much", she said and added "Come, let me cool you down a bit" and gave me a long, melting kiss. Then she grabbed my arm and ushered me inside.

* * *

On the morning of the flight, Martin and Petya had come to see us off. Martin wasn't making a big deal of it because I'd be back anyway.

Our flight was in the afternoon. While we had time, we could have coffee by Asenovgrad's creek. And we had the chance to catch the end of the morning cool. I parked the car at the edge of the centre, at a ten-minute distance on foot, so that we could walk around the centre for a while. Asenovgrad's centre was not a big one anyway.

When we got to the other end of the centre, where the shops to have coffee were plenty, we met a crowd expectable for a Saturday morning. Apparently nobody wanted to miss the coolness.

As I gazed towards the empty seats in the shops, I was also looking for familiar faces but I couldn't spot anyone, or couldn't recognize.

Still looking around, we caught a glimpse of Lee, sitting with two girls. As we approached, unnoticed, his last words to the girls were:

"OK then, check her out a little. See if she's a clean girl. After all, I'm going to marry her."

"Still on the look-out, Lee?" I asked when we got there.

"Oh yeah. There's this girl, I'm having my cousins check her out."

"At this permanence you'll find one soon, God willing."

"Forget permanence, I'll find nothing with this luck. By the way, let me introduce my cousins."

"Hi there!"

"Hi!"

Lee's cousins were sweet. Both were brunettes. Obviously local. Otherwise what business would Lee have in Asenovgrad?

"So, my man! What are you up to?" asked Lee.

"No plans, really. Just out for coffee."

"Got it. Will you go to Plovdiv later? I got some friends that make excellent soufflé. Come with me if you will. They're warm people."

"Unfortunately no, Lee. We have a plane to London in the afternoon."

"Really! I thought you would be going next week."

"Evdokiya tempted me", I said. Lee gave his ever-same smile on this.

"Then I'll say goodbye to you now Evdokiya", said Lee.

"Take good care of yourself, Lee. Let me know if you make an escapade to Russia."

"Absolutely. Say hi to your sister for me. I'll come especially to see her."

"Конечно![16] Do come, really."

"Deal" said Lee and we left them to sit at a place three buildings away.

* * *

And it was time for the trip now. Before handing over our luggage at the airport, we had stopped at the car-park for our last smoke before the journey. There were flights only to two destinations from this airport and just one plane was in sight.

"Are you going on that piece of junk?" asked Martin.

---

(16)   TN: Russian for "Of course!"

"So it seems. We'll be fine. It's just a four-hour trip", I said.

"Really! It's shorter than going to Istanbul by bus."

"Yes. But if we take into account the fact that I hate public transportation, even this is too much."

"You came here via Istanbul by car, right?"

"Exactly. Mandatory transfer, let's say. I had to stop at Istanbul to get my car on my way here from Belarus. So no matter how much I didn't like it, I had to follow this road map."

"I can guess", he said with his usual smirk.

"I'm resigning the car to you till I get back. It been lying still for a long time. Liven it up a little."

"Don't worry, clearly I'll take better care of it than you. Considering the way you drive."

"Get outta here! I'm a better driver than you."

"Of course. That's why you never miss a hole on the roads."

"I fall into them on purpose. I'm tiring the mechanics. Consider it as sweating while you work out."

"That's why you have funny noises coming from the engine. Like a tractor engine…"

"That's what I'm saying. The strong engine roars."

"Enough, shoot the bull!" interrupted Petya and went on "The trip is in half an hour. Who knows when I'll see Evdokiya again".

Smiling, we cut the nonsense and bid our farewells in turns, after our cigarettes were done with.

We checked in our luggage, went through passport control, and took our seats in the plane. I had let Evdokiya sit at the window seat. With rather meaningful eyes, she was watching the empty field that led to Plovdiv as we waited for take-off.

"I'm going to miss it here. In such a short time, we adopted memories that would rasp long years."

"Like I said before, maybe we'll coincide again, in the life of a different universe."

"Will I find you here again?

"I don't know. As a matter of fact, I wonder that myself."

"I'll write you a letter. Old school..."

"To which address?" I asked.

"I don't know. You tell me."

I looked into her eyes. There was no hope. But there was a soul begging for some hope to rise. Wanting to believe in miracles…

"If you ever happen to pass by this place again, find the glass that you set free the first night we met. You know where it is, the place of the shattered pieces at least… Burry the letter you wrote under the glass and step on it firmly and say "Greetings to a lost rambler!" Maybe… Maybe on a yet another rainy June evening my soul will meet what you've written", I said.

The aeroplane's powerful engines sprang to life, its tyres screaking the tarmac, and we sped up to the clouds. We looked down at Plovdiv. Plovdiv was telling me that it wouldn't forgive me this time if I was late again.

- 4 -

The plane landed in London; we passed through some mandatory controls and picked up our luggage.

Here I was again, at the city I was cursed in. Actually there was no great reason for this, in general. Still, when I reduced the matter to a personal level, I had plenty of reasons to cuss.

A corrupted city, where everything was attached to materialism… Like a multi-faced medallion actually. On one face, those who think they are living life to the fullest, on the other, those who suffocate inside a false utopia… The only place to live for some, and just a place to make money for others. I had known many people here; ones who had come to make money and lost another piece of their soul each passing day.

A city that took another part of your personality and replaced it with a tiny place, hardly visible to the eye, in your valet. Maybe all this is a small piece of my paranoia but after witnessing all that factitiousness, I trust my paranoia about this place more than anything else in here. Those with pathetic dreams may drown here. Totally free…

When we landed at the airport and got into London, as far as I could tell, Evdokiya had prepared everything in advance. From the place we would stay, to the places we could possibly go.

Forget it! I already knew all the limited number of quality joints that could isolate me from this place, if they were as I had left them.

Evdokiya had made a reservation at a hotel by Tower Hill for the both of us. We started off with getting settled in our room and drinking enough to prevent us from spending our time here sober. The exhibition would start in eight days and I didn't want to spend the time till then by thinking of Plovdiv. I had hit the road once again, before I could enjoy it.

At least it wasn't for long. A week or two at most… Though my one week in Plovdiv was effective enough to press a few years of my life, but a week here was just one week for me.

Neither of us had the intention to go out tonight. After going through the mini, so tiny it made you swear, refrigerator in the room, I could find a bourbon worth drinking.

We swallowed up the small bottle but it wasn't enough. We had to get out of the hotel and buy a litre from the nearest store and smuggle it in. It was better than a kick in the balls for the first night. As a small unnoticed gesture, the room had a nice view.

As I sipped from my glass, looking out the window, London City was shining with many lights. Evdokiya came by too. She took off her clothes and leaned on the large window leading to the view. Once again we were steamrolling over the night that turned into a riot of colours with the lights of the city.

* * *

In our post-morning breakfast, Evdokiya said that she would meet people from the organisation for some formality applications. Registering for the exhibition and all, the usual load of necessary rubbish.

She left me a mobile phone line and said that they would be calling from the organisation during the day. And they did.

They thanked me for my participation in the organisation. They said a few more things but I didn't turn much attention. Anyway, it was just details, spoken for the sake of conversation.

They said they would send someone to help and guide me. Even though I said it wasn't necessary at all, I agreed when they insisted so that I wouldn't have to listen any longer, then I hung up the phone.

A couple of hours later, in the evening, Evdokiya came back.

"I talked to some important people, they are very curious about the statue you'll make", she said.

"Who are they?" I asked.

"Never mind. You won't care even if I tell you. What did you do while I was gone?"

"Nothing. I've just been on the booze since you left."

"Fine. Let's go out and get something to eat. By the

way, two days later they'll be having a cocktail party for all the artists participating in the exhibition."

"Let them. What's that got to do with us?"

"You are one of the participants!"

"So what? It'll be boring. Full of cocktails and swaggerers."

"I'll come with you. We'll make it fun together."

"Deal then. But we won't stay long. There's a much better place I want to take you afterwards."

"Deal."

* * *

I could hardly wake up with the ringing of the phone. Once again we had had one too many drinks at dinner. It was as if we were here not to take part in the exhibition but to wander around drunk and peak the dipsomania index.

The phone kept buzzing. As I hardly reached for it, I saw that it was an unregistered number calling. I didn't have to answer since it wasn't Evdokiya. It hushed after a few more rings. When it started to ring again just as I had put my head back on the pillow, I answered rather angrily and called out:

"What?"

"I'm sorry. Mr Attila… Ummm… Sorry, I can't see your last name in the records."

"Never mind. I don't give out my last name to anyone. Say what you want to say so I can hang up and go back to sleep."

"Excuse me. Sorry for bother…"

"Screw that!" I had interrupted. God! How people lose themselves in work like that. "Just say what you need to say. I know you're doing your job. I respect that too, but just get on with it before tiring the both of us."

"Well. The person we sent to assist you wasn't able to reach you, he is now at the hotel lobby trying to reach you."

"There was no need. Anyway, I'll go down and meet him in a while. Cheers."

"We thank you and…"

"Bye", I said and hung up the phone. It was like they were trying to torture me. When I got down I met a guy that was Indian or Pakistani or something like that.

"Hello. You're here for me. It wasn't worth the trouble. You may leave", I said.

"Hillo. But I am heer to hilp you."

"What'd you say? Never mind now. Now listen. Give me your number. I'll call you if I need anything. Now go and chill. Don't worry, if they ask, I'll tell them you've been great help", I said.

I got his number and sent him off in due form. He had told me his name but I couldn't catch it so, playing by ear, I listed him in the phone book as 'Punjab'.

By the way, Evdokiya was missing again. When I called, she said she was in an interview with one of the organisers and that she wanted to meet outside as soon as she got out. So I told her to come directly to Shoreditch after she was finished.

I was able to have a salvo of booze till Evdokiya arrived. There was a bar I liked to go in the past. It was at the entrance of Shoreditch, on the way from Hoxton.

After getting off the intracity bus and some walking, I was at the entrance of the joint. The Bridge Bar.

As I got in, everything was as I had left them. In fact, that was its biggest selling point. From the register to its curtains, from the coffee grinders to the posters on its walls and to the numerous stuff in its decoration; it was a fully antique concept bar.

Dim lights were adjusted at a fine and successful consistence. Just like in the movies, it had an atmosphere tasting heavy, philosophical and musical. Like I could have named the place "The Mist of the Last Dance" or "Candlelight Ceremony".

It was half-full inside. The upper floor must have been choke-full as always, probably. The upper floor was designed to host large groups, decorated like a luxurious living room from the early 20th century. Anyway, I lay my eyes on a place downstairs, took my drink and sat on the bar stool.

I had finally met a quality environment since I arrived at London. People were distant but warm. I had a couple of hours to spend before Evdokiya got out.

I borrowed a pen and paper from the bartender and started scribbling for the statue I would make, while I had the time. I couldn't really think of much. I was at least very rusty at designing.

As I was sipping my drink with pleasure, for a moment I went outside for a smoke. When I came back, there were two girls sitting at the empty seat next to mine.

They were joyfully telling each other stuff and then laughing at it. The one sitting at my side was stealing glances at the things I'd scribbled. The other one blatantly…

I had finally drawn up something that was not so bad. The design consisted of a thorny ivy with a scorpion inside the rose on top of it, and naked sinners trying to climb that ivy.

Somehow, suddenly I couldn't accept the design completely. I put the lid of the pen back on and tossed it into the wooden bulge in front of me. Then I took another sip from my drink and went back outside for another smoke.

When I got back, both of the girls had craned over and were looking at my design. I got close to them and said:

"It's just some piss-arsed rubbish. Possibly out of your liking."

"We think it's nice", said the brunette.

The brunette was of medium height and warmhearted. The other was taller than her and blonde. They looked like lively people. The authenticity in their smiles was proof of that.

"Do you professionally deal in design?" asked the blonde one.

"Not really. But I can say it's related to what I do."

The blonde went on "So what do you do normally?"

"I make statues. What about you? Obviously you don't belong here."

"Splendid! So you're an artist. Well we deal with boring office work. We picked London for the weekend break", replied the brunette this time and went on:

"Where did you come here from?"

"Some place on earth. And you?"

They giggled again.

"So did we. Guess if you like."

I cased out both of them. Since I was very unskilful at guessing, I was just trying to find countries that would fit their appearance. I made the guess for the blonde one:

"You must have come from Scandinavia."

"Don't cheat. You've mentioned more than one country."

"OK then, I'll guess more specifically. I think your friend in from South America."

"That was absolutely a more definite guess", said the brunette, as they both giggled again.

The phone rang at the same time I reached for my drink. When I looked at the phone, I saw it was Evdokiya calling.

"Hello"

"Hello, Attila. I just got out."

"Good. You're coming straight here, right?

"Yes. I'll be there in half an hour. Can you pick me up at Shoreditch station?"

"OK. I'll be there soon enough."

"Deal."

After I put the phone back into my pocket, I reached at my drink to complete my previous intention. The blonde hit the glass and asked:

"The missus called and you have to go, right?"

"We could say that. That's all the same, right?

"Absolutely. After all, we're just a couple of rovers that you happened to come across in London. Perfect Strangers!"

"I agree to that. Anyway, I ask your permission for now, ladies."

"Permission granted."

I took the last sip from my glass and as I had headed for the door after putting my lighter and other stuff into my pocket, the blonde one called out behind me:

"Hey! You forgot to tell us your name, in honour of the drink."

"So did you… If we meet again, that'll be the first thing we'll talk about", I said, got out and lit a cigarette.

* * *

After we met, we got dinner out of the way at the nearest place and with Evdokiya's recommendation, we went to a retro bar in Piccadilly. Everything we did felt absurd. What were we doing here? Every day we spent here was a waste of time.

If it weren't for Evdokiya, I would have returned the same day I arrived. But now she is right in front of me and she is sipping her drink, riveting her gaze on me with those eyes that make my head spin every time I see them.

Had she hit me in a much vulnerable time? I had returned to this city, which made me curse every time I mention its name, just to prolong the inevitable for one more week.

No, no… It couldn't be that simple. Although it was crystal clear, even my mind had shackled this truth. But I have to admit to myself. She resembled Miranda very much in all but two aspects. Only Miranda had sharp ice-blue eyes and she was a little taller.

How could they be so much alike; from the shade of their hair to the softness of their lips. Not even to mention the way they talk… God was really punishing me by designating the fact of losing at the beginning. Maybe I deserved this. None of us were good. Like in the definition somebody made some day: We were lost ramblers and winning something by knowing that we would lose it, was a successful punishment for us.

Evdokiya pulled me back to reality by poking my hand and said with her eyes half squint:

"I know you won't tell me. But I really wonder what you're thinking."

"Just unimportant details not be dwelled on too much."

"So be it. By the way, the exhibition is coming up soon and you haven't even started to do anything."

"You're right. I must start tomorrow."

"OK. Tomorrow morning I'll arrange a workshop were you can start working."

"I can't work in a workshop. I have another plan for the work place.

"Tell me then."

"I'll set up a furnace for the iron, a little out of town."

"How?"

"And I need to stay there till I complete the statue. Don't worry, if all goes well, I'll finish in one night."

"Fine then, I'll allow you one night", she said, smiling. She was just trying to tidy up her hair when I raised my glass and said:

"Let them loose. I want to freeze you in my memory in the way I like to see you."

Some shyness and some innocence cast over her face. When she let her hair loose again, some part fell onto her face. It was like a shy innocent angel being lustful at the same time. She leaned over and said something in my ear that I can't tell anyone, and kissed the right side of my jaw.

"You're pushing my limits to seduce me and really wind me up, right?" I said and with my hand, I pulled aside her hair that had fallen down shyly.

"I'm just trying to inspire", she said, winking. "By the way, will you be able to take care of the setting up tomorrow? There's the cocktail party in the evening, you know".

"I will, but I'd completely forgotten about the cocktail part. I was thinking I would start working on the statue tomorrow night."

"But you promised for that cocktail party. Can't you find a way?"

"Right. Then after setting everything up, I'll come back for the cocktail party and return afterwards. If conditions are suitable I'll be finished by the dawn of the next day."

"That's better. So have you decided what you'll make?"

"Yes", I said and took out the design I had scribbled today and handed it to her.

She slowly unfolded the paper and looked at it as if reading a letter. The smile on her face broadened up. The moistness of her eye began flickering.

"отлично[17]! So beautiful. Really very beautiful. You impress me once again", she said and asked "Can you really make this in a single night?"

"Have no doubt. By the way, tomorrow I need to call

---

(17)   TN: Russian for "Excellent".

this guy who is supposedly sent to help me. He may come in handy for finding the supplies."

We got out of the place hugging each other. She was tucked under my arm. We walked all the way to the hotel like this. We said nothing. We were just feeling the presence of each other and plucking, from where the night had hidden them, pieces of serenity that would die out by morning.

* * *

I had set the alarm and woken up out of my biological clock for the first time in a long while. After getting over the revival part, the first thing I did was to call this assistant guy.

"Good morning Punjab. How are you?"

"Good morning Mr. Attila. I am fine. How are you? My name is not Punjab, by the way."

"Look I don't really understand you. Anyway, we have lots to do today. You may be useful. I'm waiting for you at the hotel. The sooner you can come, the better."

"OK. I'm leaving in a minute."

I started to get ready till he came. While choosing where I'd settle and thinking of how to do the set-up, I was also putting together the list of material I needed for this. When Evdokiya woke up and saw this, her mood lifted. She was proud of both me and herself. It hadn't been easy to bring me back and she was aware of her success.

Half an hour later Punjab arrived. We dashed out without waiting. The guy couldn't even understand what was going on, or what would happen. I told him I would explain on the way and firstly, we went to rent a pick-up truck.

At the place where we rent the pick-up, I slipped the list that I had prepared into his hand and started to go over it verbally:

"Look Punjab. These are the necessary materials. A comfortable camping tent, enough bricks for me to build a wall as big as the tent, and hard coal to burn, a generator, an audio system, a mini fridge, couple of torches, an anvil, mould iron and some junk iron, building and workshop tools to do the job and a litre of Kumis[18]."

"Koumish?

"No. Kumis. Look it up a little. Now let's choose a pick-up that we can fit all this stuff into. Then we'll start getting the material."

After checking out the trucks for a while, even if I wasn't fully satisfied, I had found a one with the steering wheel on the left. I couldn't find it bearable to add an opposite side steering wheel to the torture of the traffic flowing on the opposite side.

Partly thanks to my forcing, we gathered everything needed in four hours. I must hand it to him, Punjab did a good job too. If it hadn't been too hard for him to find the Kumis, we could have finished earlier but even this was faster than I had expected.

After sending off Punjab, thanking him and telling him I could handle the rest on my own, I drove to an empty field about one hour away from London. First I quickly took care of setting up everything but the furnace,

---

(18) A fermented drink made from mare's milk, common among peoples of the Central Asian steppes.

and took a bottle of whiskey from the mini fridge and began the opening.

The furnace had taken more time than I expected. It was cloudy and darkness was about to fall but I was finished. The sky being cloudy was a condition better than my expectations. I at least needed a drizzling rain.

After taking care of everything swiftly and functionally, all there was left to do was going back and getting the cocktail party out of the way. Even if I had taken a small amount of alcohol, this was London and I had had enough to have problems with the alcoholmeter. Driving more carefully, I arrived at the hotel 20 minutes later than I had thought.

* * *

When I got in the room Evdokiya was completely ready and was scowling at me.

"I was expecting you earlier. Hurry up or we'll be late", she said.

"I'm sorry, моя звёздочка. It was a little challenging."

"Did you drink? I had prepared something to drink for you, too", she said and sloshed down one of the glasses on the table. Then handing me other one, she added "C'mon speed yourself up. I prepared your clothes. They're on the bed."

I had showered quickly and got ready. God, women can really be autocratic, no matter how calm they may seem... After getting dressed and going to Evdokiya, I had suddenly realised what I couldn't realise in the first place because of the haste. She was wearing a very gorgeous wine-coloured dress. As she turned around when she saw me coming, her golden hair which she had let wavy, fell onto the shoulders of her dress.

The angel's wings had spread once again. Stars were falling and crashing into each other; and another slap, stunning my soul, was coming down. I started wiggling inside. It was as if the volcano inside me was roaring again. Then, reading me like an open book, Evdokiya said:

"The night is just beginning, мой герой. Let's wait for the hour and minute hands to race each other", and headed for the door after giving me a kiss that made me tide between the real and surreal.

Punjab was waiting for us outside, holding the door of a luxury car.

"I will be your driver tonight", he said, laughing heartily. I was getting to like this guy.

When we arrived at the place where the party was held, we met a crowd that was not so large. I assume they had been quite choosy. Still, it was full of swaggerers in suits. Evdokiya took my arm and said:

"Don't worry, I won't push you so much. First we'll just say hello to a few people who want to meet you. Then we're on our own", and she kept her word. After stepping in, we had some chat with some of the owners of the organisation on general and significant issues. One of them had said that he was there at my previous exhibition.

After suffocating a bit in the elite atmosphere I dreaded, drinks were served. I would have cut it short if it hadn't been short. The drinks consisted of soft cocktails. I don't like cocktails! I'm a stable drinker. Certain things… But I was able to get my hands on some wine after tipping the waiter.

At least the jazz musicians made the night more bearable. People's faces were covered with make-believe or flamboyant smiles. But Evdokiya was so astonishing that I was able to overlook all of this without difficulty.

At one time, Evdokiya went to the restroom and I looked around when I was alone. Suddenly two girls caught my eye. These were the girls I had seen at The Bridge Bar. I took my glass and went over to them. Hitting theirs' with mine, I said:

"My name is Attila, ladies. As promised, I'm picking up from the topic of our last encounter."

They giggled again and the blonde one told me their respective names:

"I am Sadie and my friend is Susana."

"Pleasure. Now I can make a more productive guess. You are from Norway and your friend is Argentinian."

"One out of two", said Susana, the brunette. "I'm from Mexico. But you were close. I appreciate that."

"I wasn't expecting to meet again so soon. Are you taking part in the exhibition too?"

"We were expecting it after seeing your drawing. One of the organisers is a close friend."

"That was even more unexpected", I said and asked to be excused after clinking glasses again, and returned to my table. I didn't want Evdokiya to misunderstand and they were quite aware of this.

Evdokiya came back with someone beside her. It was Valeria. The chains of coincidence were outright messing around with me tonight.

"Look who I ran into", said Evdokiya.

When I left my drink on the table in front of me and headed for the exit, Valeria held my arm and laughing, she said:

"You joker. Aren't you glad you saw me? Wait, I haven't done anything to make you run away yet."

"I'm just running away from tonight's surprises", I said, half joking.

"One's fears come true. Maybe it will be a night with more surprises", she said and took a sip from the glass I'd left on the table. "Hmm… I guess the wine is special for you only."

"We didn't even think we would meet you here", said Evdokiya.

"I didn't want to tell you. I'll have a painting in the exhibition."

"Congratulations, then. Which way is your table?" I asked, to send her off.

When she attached herself, saying "As a matter of fact, I don't have a specific table. I can join you", I couldn't get any ruder or dismiss her, so I invited her perforce.

This situation had made Evdokiya pretty uncomfortable. I, since I hadn't wanted to come in the first place, had left the flow of everything to Evdokiya. My only concern was for time to move quickly and give an end to this cocktail party.

As the girls went on talking, their words became sharper. Evdokiya was getting nervous because she was having to put up with the ego of an arrogant idiot. Valeria was furious because she wasn't getting the attention she expected.

Even if they weren't directing the sharp words to each other, they could make it quite evident in a roundabout way. The topic was no longer me, it had turned into a battle of overtopping between the girls. Oh, women! The sharpness of their claws matched each other's when the conditions allowed. It is one of the oldest known unsolved puzzles; what women really want. So I don't even want to bother with this.

At one time, Valeria left us, asking permission to go to the ladies' room. After her, Evdokiya sighed with relief.

"Wow! How brazen this woman has become since last time", she said.

"Lot of pamperers she has."

"So the rules of nature apply. Monkeys jump onto anything shiny without thought, no matter how worthless it is."

"You put the lid on it nicely", I said.

"Anyway, I won't let such silly things dispirit me. I'm going out for a smoke", she said and, taking her purse, she headed for the front door.

As soon as Evdokiya went out, Sadie and Susana came by with pompous hand clapping.

"Wow! You can manage two girls at the same time, side by side. Even when the both don't take a look from the outside and fight for you. What more surprises do you have?" said Susana.

"Don't say surprise to me. Besides, it's not want you think."

"Yeah sure. It's never how it looks."

Valeria came in as I was saying "Look…"

"My, my! You turned out to be even faster and shameless than I thought. It appears you're interested in any girl but me."

"Valeria! It's not what you think"

"It never is", Valeria said, smiling.

"That's what we said", added Susana.

Valeria put her hand on my waist and said "Come, let's go to my room and let's talk this over in a way that is not as it looks. Or do you not find me beautiful enough to talk? You should take a closer look".

"Don't get it personal, you are quite pretty but the frequencies are different and you've had a bit too much to drink", I said. Then, as I made a stop sign with my hand and starting "Look girls…" the second slap came and Evdokiya came by.

"What's going on here?"

The genie was out of the bottle. God help us all! I took a mouth embittering sip from my drink and said:

"Look Evdokiya. It's not what… Whatever, the situation looks complicated but actually it's simple."

"Right, very simple", interrupted Valeria, "Inside your man, is a stud enough for a whole herd".

"Don't be silly. You're getting drunk", I said.

Valeria rushed in "What? You've started sneakily sniffing all the flowers except me. You're just playing hard to get for me".

When I said "Look Evdokiya, these ladies had made comments on my design while I was drawing it at the bar before I got here. Now we just ran into each other here", Evdokiya looked at the girls. Only when the girls nodded in my approval, did her scowled eyes loosen.

"What about me?" interrupted Valeria again "You can't deny you want me".

"You're drunk. Get a grip of yourself."

Valeria took her glass from the table together with mine, stretched it out to me and after taking a sip from hers, she said:

"I am fine. You pull yourself together. See, you are with people that look like a saddle on a sow. While I… Open your eyes. Everyone is after me."

Evdokiya just kept silent and looked at me. She had believed Valeria's poisonous words. She adopted it like an inevitable truth. I could read it in her eyes. She talked about all our talks. She remembered the predictable darkness that I kept buried inside, that I refrained from telling. I could see her eyes filling with tears. She was as if boiling to hit my heart, like an acid flood overflowing the dam of fortitude. She was offended, humiliated. And her acceptance of this humiliation was on a thin line.

She couldn't stand any longer and took her purse and headed for the exit. After a few steps, she turned and looked back for a moment, for seconds that divided time into segments. Her eyes were really flickering and their blueness challenging Miranda's.

I sloshed down my glass and after looking into her Evdokiya's flickering eyes, feeling them, I turned to Valeria.

"In a few years, the beauty of your face, your body will pass and you will open your eyes as a pathetic person, still consoling herself with the obsession of old days. In case prostitution has stuck onto your soul, your change will be no more than a painted slut that nobody deigns to. So in short, beauty passes, floozy stays. So sober up from the drunkenness of your current beauty honey, and get rid of the flattery of your arrogance already", I said and gave her the empty glass, turned my back to her and started walking on the glided road set before me, flowing from Evdokiya's eyes.

In my each step, the blueness of Evdokiya's eyes became sharper and her eyes, which were proud of me, flickered even more. She took my arm when I reached her and closed her eyes, taking a deep breath that justified her not feeling remorse.

* * *

We took a short walk after leaving the place and then went to The Bridge Bar. It was time to cheer Evdokiya up and focus on the job of the night. Some waking had already been good for Evdokiya.

"This place is nice. How did you find it?" she asked after cheering up some more.

"An old memory, I could say. By the way, I'm glad you didn't get carried away with tonight's bullshit."

"Would I let some useless person cast a shadow on our last times together? It happened there and it's over. Actually, I even pitied her drunkenness afterwards", she said and put her hand in her purse. After fumbling in it for a while, she took out a silver rosette.

"I want to give this to you. It is an ancient symbol of where I come from and only a few people in the world have one. You'll remember me; as a blurry memory, almost a reality once."

She put the rosette in front of me and pushed it over

to me. First I looked at her face meaningfully. Then as I reached out to take the rosette, she held my hand.

"Go now, мой герой. Seduce me once more with what you create tonight", she said. She placed the rosette into my extended hand and closed my fingers, put a kiss on it, like a seal.

I headed for my camping place once more as it came closer to midnight. The sky was cloudy but without rain. The only thing I asked for along the way was for the rain to drizzle, even if a little bit. But with a successful misfortune, not even a single drop fell until I got there.

When I arrived, I quickly changed my clothes and put on my leather apron, I put five strong torches around my area and lit them, placed my anvil by the furnace and lit the furnace too, set up my audio system and turned on the Psychedelic Rock songs that echoed in the nature, took out my bourbon from the mini fridge, and starting waiting for the first rain to start drizzling.

The night was flowing by but not a single drop of rain was falling. I was flaring up the furnace once in a while and separating the metal pieces for the attachments in the design, consuming the night together with my drink.

* * *

By dawn, I had dozed off, being also drowsed by the furnace. It was past noon when I woke up. The torches had died down, the furnace weakened and the bottle had seen the bottom.

There, it was the rain's fault. If it had rained again last night, in this land where it is never absent, maybe I would have woken up with a beautiful piece of art this morning. Anyway, what was done was done. At least I could go back to the city and refresh my unwillingly depleted drink. And, I would have a chance to have coffee with Evdokiya.

I set off towards the city without waiting and it was close to the end of the afternoon when I arrived. I called Evdokiya as soon as I stopped the pick-up at the hotel car park.

"Hello, Evdokiya."

"Hello, did you finish? I can't wait to see it immediately", she said in a cheerful voice.

"Wait, don't rush. The damn rain didn't fall and I could do nothing."

"What! Get back to work right away then."

"I came back to the city to fill up my supplies. I thought we could have coffee together before I go back."

"Not before you finish. I am out of bounds for you until you are done. Now go back and make the statue that we will celebrate tomorrow! See you."

"Your words are my command! I'll see you tomorrow then", I said and hung up the phone, smiling.

Even if after a long time, for once, I had to do what I had to do. I made myself adopt the idea and after supplying my drink, I headed towards my camping place on the road north. That was a bit ironic. I had been thrown in the North again, without knowing it.

On my way north, as I passed Finsbury Park, I suddenly thought of someone here. The name being not so important, he had a hard-to-get musical archive and always gave me albums that contained songs that I needed, or would need.

I stopped in front of the shop and I was greeted with a cold longing as soon as I got in. He had an ill humour but he also had the feature of being able to read all souls after talking for a while. When I told him that I would be forging iron for a statue, he stopped me with an obvious gesture and disappeared. After ferreting around for more than a quarter hour, he came back with an album of shaman music in hand and said that this would be useful, and sent me off again with a cold attitude.

Everything was over before I knew it and I went out with what I got, without giving it much thought. Walking easy and clear, a sensation arouse in me as I reached the truck and I looked around rather meaningfully towards the road.

The number 29 bus was approaching. When I scanned the bus before getting into the pick-up, a silhouette inside it stuck in my eye like a bullet. Time suddenly came to a complete halt. My muscles drained away, my veins began to split and everything but the silhouette in the bus became blurry. My heart beats were the only sounds in the world. I was burning. My veins were full of boiling blood and my eyes were filling up with an insane pressure. God, had I come to this point finally? Had she driven me to the point of madness where I began seeing illusions?

While the bus flowed before my eyes like a movie strip, the moment my soul began to reject this reality, I felt the pain of a magic arrow sticking into my heart. The arrow had come from ice-blue gazes that chilled my soul and stuck the reality, which I tried to deny, into the only crack in my heart. Even as I was ready to believe the impossible, I could not perceive this as reality; until the ice-blue eyes shook the world with the only looks that could see me… Right at that time, I was able to accept that this was the utter truth. A look from Miranda's ice-blue eyes, slowly surrounding my entire existence, had frozen all real and unreal perceptions.

Senselessly, my body loosened and when our eyes met, just a single word eluded everything and assumed the body that echoed in the universe:

"Goddess!"

* * *

The steering wheel was getting out of control as I sped up. I was having trouble gaining control over my trembling hands and I was still thinking that this was a hallucination, wanting to accept it that way. Because if it were real, I was not sure if I could bear the consequences that would come from this.

"I had chosen impossible dreams; she, the freedom of fake desires", I murmured to myself and barely lit a cigarette with my still trembling hands.

Disconnections in the concept of time began to occur. I couldn't even understand how I got to my camping place. I had knocked down my tent as I made an unintentional speedy entrance and tried to park.

I could not stand still because of the boiling in my veins. I was being prevented from cooling down. I hurried out of the pick-up, lit the torches and started flaring up the furnace once again. When the coal met the eye-brightening yellow like a volcanic vent, suddenly I felt an unexpected coolness on my head. A rain drop had fallen.

This was the sign that said it was the time now. Just like what had happened today... I started playing the music album, I fed the raw iron into the flared up furnace, put on my leather apron and took a long, throat-lacerating sip from the new bottle. My ceremony was beginning.

I could feel the slow but plumpy raindrops sliding from my body. The torches were making my sledgehammer shine and with slow steps, as if going to officiate a strong rite, I approached the anvil. Without knowing it, I had become furious. I was hurting, I was angry and at the same time I was being celebrated.

I took the brand, shining like gold, out of the furnace and took it to the anvil. Raindrops evaporated as they fell on it, creating small instantaneous black spots on the iron where they landed. I raised my sledgehammer to the sky and with the shaman's beating of the drum in the music, I brought it down on the brand like a thunderbolt.

My strikes came down synchronous with the rhythm of the drums. After a few strikes, I reached out to my bottle and took a sip, poured some on the hot iron and put it back in the furnace. I was going on like this. As the alcohol increased, I noticed the adrenalin becoming more evident in my veins. My cognisance ability was weakening and I was splitting the rainy night with the sounds of metals meeting.

I kept on striking. I forged the booze and the music into the brand's soul until the morning light dominated the earth. I grew stronger as I hit and I hit again. I was sculpting the tiniest details and then striking its body unceasingly. My sweat was mixed with the falling rain, and my ecstatic self was derangedly dancing to the music. I was hitting relentlessly as if I had entered the dimension of the never-ending song.

As the lights of the new day began to wash over the clouds, I landed my final strike as if challenging the lightning, poured Kumis on the already cooling iron and raised its sizzles, its final sounds, to the sky.

The day's lights walked slowly on the ground. As they moved on to surround me, I was standing with my sledgehammer in hand, trying to look at my piece of work with eyes that saw the rocking world. When the light reached my body, I let my hammer slip from my hand and kneeled down to watch the light dancing on my work.

I saw a steppe cavalry sabre with a horsehead damask on its haft, when my work granted audience to the light and revealed itself to me. I never thought about or questioned its existence.

I raised up, took a firm grip on the sword's handle, kept it straight up and examined it before roaring and sticking it into the ground. The rite was over, everything else left behind had become meaningless. I looked at the rocking sword's haft, shouldered my sledgehammer and moved with the thoughts of the place I belong, leaving everything else behind. The sunlight was caressing my left cheek, as if consoling me.

- 5 -

I woke up to the lurching of the plane while landing. Plovdiv's noon sun was hitting me in the face from the small window of the aeroplane. When I got out as soon as the plane stopped, Plovdiv's air moved deeply into my lungs, filling me with some hope and some sadness.

Evdokiya was not there when I returned to the hotel before catching the plane, and I had taken my things and returned to Plovdiv on the forenoon flight without saying anything to anyone. Probably Evdokiya will spend most of her time hating me for this. I can't blame her. All in all, I was one of the lost ramblers.

I was feeling very tired and there was nobody to meet me because I had not told them. I took a taxi and went deliberately to Asenovgrad city centre. Like on the day I first arrived, I wanted to go home without a purpose, without hurry. From the centre to home, I walked slowly until I got there. I had had too many smokes for the distance. As I blew the smoke of each of them, I was watching it blow past my shoulders, imagining my tiring thoughts disappearing with them.

When I got inside my house, I went straight to the kitchen without even taking off my shoes, and took the quarter-full bottle of bourbon, which I found after some searching, to my bedroom. I got half-naked and dropped myself into the armchair. When I lifted my head while taking a sip from the bottle, I saw the forbidden chest.

It was a tiny chest, full of memories from Miranda. After losing her I had put everything into it before getting lost myself. I hadn't dared to open it after the day I had closed it. Maybe now was the time to open it.

After hesitantly tiding between the possibilities some more, I lit a cigarette and got up after taking a sip from the bottle. I tended towards the table and turned on the song she liked to listen to; Billy Idol's 'Rebel Yell'. Then I took the chest, the size of a human head, in my hands and stared at it for a while.

I, too, had grown fond of this song with her. Now she's gone and I'm listening to it alone. I listened till the end of the song, remembering her face, her voice and her smell. So distinct, so lethal…

I put out my cigarette when the song ended and looked once more to the closed chest in my hand. I had to do this now. What more could slip from my hands, when I had already lost the ones I had feared I would lose?

I took the key that hanged from its handle. Then slowly and carefully, I unlocked the chest. My eyes started to fill as I slowly opened the lid. I let myself go. I let everything go and when I lifted the lid, I saw some of our old smiling photographs, the letter she wrote and gave to me, tickets of concerts we went to, a broken guitar pick, miniature bottles of my favourite drinks and the old juke box.

One of my teardrops made a run for it and fell onto the letter at the top. After wiping the remaining ones with the back of my thumb, I took the music box and wound it up. Then I placed it onto the table, lifted the cover and set the melody free. The music was dancing inside the room together with my thoughts that reminisced the past. I sipped from my drink once more, lit another cigarette and could only watch this duo. They went on mesmerising my shackled teardrops, melancholically flirting with each other. I was just honouring the smoke of this dance with the one coming out of my cigarette.

Everything was so hard. If I let myself go, I suffocated; if I struggled, I sank deeper into the depth of old memories. The most of it had turned into a blurry dream but lanced my feelings with its sharpness. Even the jukebox was ashamed of the sorrow in its sound, while looking into my bloody eyes.

After winding up the music box many times and reading all the old letters, I felt the deep void in me once again. The bottomless pit… The darkness I jumped into willingly, and in which I'm still falling, going deeper and deeper…

I took a look at the old photos from the chest, then I put all the memories, with which I have communed with one by one, back into the chest and put the key in my pocket. Later I got out and began walking towards Asenova Krepust. Darkness had fell, translucent clouds had covered a part of the blue full moon.

As it was a steep hill, I could go up to Asenova Krepust only after walking for a half-hour. It was closed for visitation at this hour. I illegally went in by jumping over the fences at the entrance and went all the way to the peak point. I came to the edge and looked at Asenovgrad with mournful eyes. The wind was blowing warm and calmly. A precipice was spread under my feet.

I moved my feet to the very edge that lead to the cliff and tried to see the bottom of the void that drowned in the darkness. Although the sky was partly cloudy, the puckish of the sky were quite bright tonight. The stars which got through from behind the clouds were lighting up the night, playing like fairies; the full moon that dominated the dark night was sitting in its throne like a queen, conducting this musical.

I didn't know what to do. I just couldn't take my eyes off the glamour of this musical. The melody of the music box was still echoing in my ears and the darkness began gradually turning into a tranquil sea. This musical must have been my initiation ceremony. On one side, I was being invited to tranquillity. But on the other side, a fickle world awaited me to extirpate the redemption of my sins.

"Fuck!" I cursed at the dark void and released the key I took from my pocket into the deepness, turned my back and headed back home. There will never be peace but I can't give up on the resolution of challenging life. Just like all the other lost ramblers…

* * *

I left the house with the late morning light and went to a cosy joint called KoShiPraim, in the middle of Asenovgrad, and after having six espressos till noon,

I headed for Plovdiv. Coffee and smokes caused small throbs but it would probably settle down soon.

As I got out of Asenovgrad, the sun was diagonally hitting the hills to my left. There was the liveliness of a nature sketch and it didn't let even a small chance of feeling regret for being here. While going to Seven, the broadness of the day was slowing down the tempo of the whole rush of life. I lit a cigarette. The breeze coming in from the half-open window was tearing pieces of ash from my cigarette.

When I reached Place of Seven Sins, Seven opened the door and looked at my face with a questioning look, then let me in with his hand on my shoulder for consolation. As I stretched out on his couch, he was trying to wash his face and sober up. Soon after, he came to me.

"You returned earlier than I thought. I was going to come to pick you up yesterday but since you didn't let know, I thought you'd want to be left alone", he said.

When I said "You're right. Yesterday I came back in such a hurry that nobody could notice. How did you know I returned?" he lifted one eyebrow and smiled like an illusionist, proud of his mystique. It was an enough answer.

As he went on saying "By the way, horsehead was a good choice. But you've made its brows too scowling", I didn't even want to be startled. Just a "But how?!" came out unwillingly from my mouth. When he again lifted his brow and smiled, I couldn't dare go on.

"Let's forget these now, Attila. There is an important matter that we need to talk about, or rather, that you need to deal with."

"I'm listening", I said.

"Prut is hell bent. He is getting ready to fight one last time in the cage."

As soon as I asked "I wasn't expecting that. Still, it's not something he hasn't done before. What do I deal with?" he hit on the answer quickly:

"He found the guys responsible for Zed's death. He'll fight against them", and I suddenly had a rude awakening. Seven lit a cigarette and went on:

"You're the one who got him out of Izgrev. So you have to deal with this. Besides, he won't listen to anyone else."

"He won't listen to me either. Like you don't know that", I said and lit a cigarette for myself.

"Still, he has a different attitude with you. And besides, don't forget that he owes you."

I tended to the bar and opened a beer for myself. It did good over the heat of the day. After cooling a bit, I wiped the beer from my lips with my thumb and turned towards Seven.

"OK, fine. I'll go to Izgrev tonight and talk to him."

"No. You can't find him there."

"Then where do I find him?"

"It's impossible to find him during the day but he spends his nights at Grebna Baza."

"Understood. I'll take care of it tonight. I'll leave now. I want to visit Atanas and Teodora."

I took two cigarettes from Seven's packet, put one behind my ear and headed to the door. Seven had also gotten up with me. Just as I opened the door, he held my arm and said:

"There is not much time, Attila. Make sure to take care of it tonight."

I threw my hand over his shoulder and bit my lip, as if cursing fate. Right then I felt Seven relaxing a little.

* * *

Atanas and Teodora were ones of us. Also, Atanas and Seven were brothers. And Teodora his wife… They were a crackpot doctor couple. Atanas was a swart and brave man, Teodora an elegant lady. Like Seven, they lived their lives in their own world and had already filled their quota for people they would deal with. The only difference; Atanas had bounced off the goal post just before getting lost like us. More accurately, Teodora had taken him from a deep purposelessness and brought him to light. Although they lived high, they were smart enough to push winning the Nobel Prize. In fact they did push…

Seven had a benign tumour and they had aimed to remove it with herbal combinations based on alternative medicine. But they had a small complication about this: All the herbs they collected from nature were either stimulants or had mellowing side effects, and their only test subject was Seven.

Whatever they tried, they couldn't get close to the result they wanted. It was impossible for them to reach a steady outcome with a single person's metabolism, and then they started to use themselves and us as willing test subjects. Still the result was the same. The only thing that happened was that everyone was walking around high, medically appropriate and healthy. In fact Martin still resents them for that. They were also angry at Martin's impassivity but they all loved each other. It was just a friendly rebuff.

At one time, in order to analyse the biological effects, they had taken Seven to Amsterdam just because medical marihuana was legal. Our guys got to see the place using this as an excuse. Zed had loved it there the most. As I had Miranda, I couldn't leave her alone and join them on this trip. They returned to Plovdiv destitutely when the result was again a bust. Actually Teodora had claimed that she had found the solution later on, but when the great disaster hit at that time, we had all dispersed without seeing the result.

I found them as I had left them; joyous, cleansed, unable to stop bickering with each other; no matter how much they cursed at it, still impatient to wait even for a minute to return to Plovdiv when they got out;, still working on their herbs and seeing that the meaning of life is in living it. We talked at length. We reminisced old times and saluted the moments impossible to break off. They were quite delightful with my return. They made this very evident and invited me into this delight.

We told each other what we did during the time we didn't see each other, mutually offered advises on these, full of 'if only's. I became increasingly full of serenity. I realized once again a truth that I was proud of. There were three roofs under which I felt truly at home: My coffin in Asenovgrad, Place of Seven Sins, and Atanas and Teodora's house.

Even though the wistful conversations couldn't even get close to cooling down, darkness was setting in. I told them about what I had heard from Seven today and that I was there to stay, and only after being forced to prove that I would be visiting again in a couple of days, I asked for their permission. Then I peacefully headed for Grebna Baza.

* * *

Grebna Baza was acting as a huge pool where rowing races were held and as an artificial lake where people went to chill. It especially had a lot of visitors while under the reign of hot weather; from those who came to exercise by running to those of all ages, trying to enjoy the evening.

I parked the car at its entrance and started walking. It could take about an hour to walk all around it. So I was moving along the waterfront, hoping that Prut would be lazy. As I approached the bridge at the middle, the number of people decreased. When the people passing by became less frequent, I lit a cigarette and as I was trying to make out the path in front of me, I heard a rugged voice from my left side.

"Hey you! What are you looking for around here?"

When I turned my head, I saw a dark body on a bench, on which no light shone. The only thing disrupting the darkness was his cigarette, which blazed as he puffed. I had found him without difficulty, earlier than I thought. I went over and shook hands firmly. As I tried to settle down on the empty place beside him, he grasped the bottle of wine he had put there.

"Not that anything would happen to you but the wine

would be wasted", he said. "Apparently you're here for me on purpose".

"I heard about the things you set about in my absence. I wanted to come after you and make you give it up", I said and grabbed the wine from his hand and took a sip.

He took the wine back in the same way and said "You've come for nothing".

When I asked "How did you find the guys?" he sloshed down the wine, spilling it from the corners of his mouth and threw his arm over the back side of the bench and answered as if it were something ordinary:

"I made a deal that would satisfy a filthy guy who arranges illegal fights. And he immediately found them for me. You'll ask anyway so I'll just tell you the deal and we can get on with it".

"Go on then."

"I'll be one against both. He'll have all the money whether I win or lose. As it is illegal, the possibility of death is at liberty and they pay handsomely. Moreover, I sold my car and placed a bet on myself on his behalf. If I win, he takes it all. That's how I convinced him."

"What did you do? You're driving me mad."

"I puffed on the dusty shelves and remembered the impossible dreams I had left there. Just like you told me to…"

"Prut!" I raised my voice.

He suddenly got up and stood on top of me, roaring "This revenge will be taken, Attila. No matter how".

Growing impatient, I got up too and yelled "Then I'll fight with you". Our faces were both full of fury. We were looking at each other like two locked manslayers.

"And we'll be two against two", I went on.

"No, Attila. The deal is done already. Otherwise the bets on me wouldn't be so high."

"I will not send you alone. You are under my responsibility."

"And Zed's revenge in under my responsibility", he retorted in sequence.

"When is the fight?"

He took a sip from the wine bottle in his hand and handed it over to me and said "Tomorrow night".

"Damn!" I said, grasped the bottle in his hand and tossed it into the dark waters of Grebna Baza.

"The bottles you throw bode no good", Prut said, smiling bitterly. The possibility of him being right made me shiver inside for a moment.

I took him by the nape, knocked our heads together and said "I'll be with you tomorrow. No matter how".

Then I held his shoulder for a moment and started walking back towards the half-lit path I had come from. The only thing I could do was to go to Apartment 101 and start drinking. Just like when trying to get Prut out of Izgrev, but this time to get him in…

* * *

When I arrived at Apartment 101, I finally found my seat vacant. I took my place without wandering around and then got my drink. My place could have been snatched even in a few minutes of opportunity. And I was right. Soon after I began sipping my drink, the hatted guy who always took my place arrived. He was with the tall beautiful girl I had seen the first time. He flashed a disturbing glance when he saw that I had taken the place before him; and they took the adjacent table.

After smiling with victory and making certain of my place, I went out onto the balcony for a smoke. It was a drowsy and tired Plovdiv evening. The lull of the half-hazy evening made all my muscles sway. I listened to the low noise of the city, as the alcohol blended with my blood. The mystic inertia of the park across me was unsettling my senses. It was as if the park's lights were intensifying and shaping into a body, giving life to Plovdiv's portrait.

This was what I had seen many times before, what I interpreted as the hidden soul of Plovdiv. It did not speak. Just like I watched it, it watched me from a distance. But it was not always visible. It would only appear at times when it sensed my lack of joy and gave birth to nice ideas that would eliminate this deprival, and tonight was the first time it revealed itself since I came back to Plovdiv.

I put out my cigarette and headed straight to my table, gathered my stuff and decided to hang out in Plovdiv nights old style. When I reached my table, the hatted place-taker at the next table was telling something to the girl across him with serious gestures. What I could hear clearly while taking my cigarette box from my table was that he said "We are just plastering emotional cracks. Nobody is building new walls".

I jumped into the car and began flushing the night, aimlessly and swiftly. As it was not a large one, I was hopping around popular bars and similar places at opposite ends of the city, giving way to the positivity of nightlife, which made you forget. People were cheerful at the places I went. They were not dwelling on the issue that much. They were drinking a bit and having simple and plain fun with the music played in the joints.

Finally I returned to Apartment 101 for a nightcap. It had livened up pretty much inside. When I couldn't find a place to sit, I went over to an empty bar stool between two ladies. When she saw the barmen pouring a triple bourbon and sliding the glass over to me as soon as I arrived, before I said anything, the woman on my left, whom the glass slid by, was quite surprised.

"Wow! Drinks coming as soon as you arrive", she said, turning towards me.

She was even more surprised when I slurred over it with a simple joke "Special for subscribers".

"They have subscription here?" she asked, taking me seriously. When I turned to look, I saw a brunette chick closing in on her twenties. In fact I was not over 30 myself. I seemed to know the chick but without dwelling on it too much, I said:

"Go back to having fun, kid. A night with a hidden moon is passing."

"That's OK. I like hiding in the darkness too. By the way, have we met before?"

"Everyone who's been here has met me."

"Why are you freezing me off? I'm just trying to have a proper conversation with you. You look like someone to be curious of and I want to discover new things."

I looked at her face again. She was obviously taller than I. Apparently she was one who approached novelties clumsily, who tasted the beauty of differences more freshly.

"Are you a student?" I asked.

"Yes. Or don't you drink with a student?"

"Usually I don't drink with anyone."

"Then you should give it a try. So what are you doing in this town? Your accents says you're not from around here."

"I came to confess my sins and pay their redemptions."

"So you've had a past here before."

"A past which also constitutes my future…"

"Maybe you'd like to tell to a stranger", she said with a sweet smile. When she asked "It's a little crowded in here. Shall we go some place more quiet?" I couldn't find any reason to turn it down.

We left and got a bottle of wine, and moved into the light beam, floating in the mist of the central park across us. Then we settled on a not-so-busy bench and as two strangers, who knew nothing of each other, we got strangeness gradually out of the way until the mist of the night met dawn.

* * *

The sun had risen but we were still in the park. Her name was Simona. We had gotten over with the bottle and even though I had lent her my jacket, she had shrank and cuddled up with the morning cool, burying her head on the left side of my chest. We had been well-behaved people all night. We had just shared our stories and tried to be cleansed, confessing our sins. The troubles one would tell to an unknown stranger.

Actually she had kissed my lips and I had answered it, in the moments when the wine got redder, but there was no passion. Or emotion… It was in the portrait of a thank you, that kiss. She was betrayed and I had lost big time. There was no compensation or consolation for either of us. There was just the warmth of the pains. That kiss had come to life with our pain, with our pain being listened to. Until the travailing of the dawn, we took turns at telling and listening. Under different circumstances I would have assumed the rambler that I am, but no matter what, I could not go as low as taking advantage of a lady's pain.

Then her eyelids separated. The tears in her eyes had still not dried out and she continued to sniffle. I rubbed her head and said:

"Precious are teardrops. Just like love… Show them only to the people who can see the brilliants inside them, every single drop". A smile that showed her relaxation covered her face and she closed her eyes again.

As the day kicked off, people had slowly began the flow of life. Simona was resisting to compose herself, rubbing my chest with her head like a cat, trying to reach a comfortable position. An old couple passed by, then a few adolescent runaways…

I was trying to take out a cigarette in my jacket's pocket without disturbing her. Before I could reach the packet, two familiar faces caught my eye. Martin and Lee were approaching us with coffee in the plastic cups in their hands. My hand was still trying to reach the pocket of the jacket that was on Simona. When Martin saw that, he asked "Oh, Attila. Are you feeling your breakfast?"

Right after him, Lee left no room for conversation when he said "Don't questions the man's fantasies, bil". Simona was half awakened with this conversation when I threw a kick to Martin from where I sat and gave Lee the fig sign and sent them off, saying "We'll talk later" in a way not to wake Simona up completely. But Simona's sleep was disturbed.

She couldn't gather herself despite her sleep being lost. I picked her up in my arms, took her to my car, which was not so far away, and took her to the address I could barely get out her mouth. Then I took her up to her apartment and got in with the key I took out of her purse, and lay her to bed. Afterwards I got out without leaving any signs. Probably we would never meet again but the peace of having spent an innocent night had covered my heart. I called Martin as soon as I got in the front door.

"Hello, Martin. What ridiculous guys you are."

"Absolutely. We've taken after you obviously", he said, laughing.

"It's not time to joke now. Did you hear about Prut's situation?"

"Yes I heard. In fact I was there when he told about it at Place of Seven Sins, but you tell me your situation first. Why didn't you tell me you were back from London?"

"It was an unexpected return. I think I saw Miranda."

"Whoa!"

"Whatever, screw me for now. I couldn't stop Prut. There is no turning back now."

"I understand. He's one wacky guy! Come to me, let's talk about this."

"No way. I'm full today. Let's gather at Place of Seven Sins and go directly from there."

"OK, I'll let the guys know. Anyway, I have nobody to call but Lewon, Mehov and Atanas and Teodora."

After suggestively asking "Were Lewon and Mehov still here? Wonder why I didn't know about that?" I warned him saying "OK call them all but tell Teodora not to come. Prut is hell bent. I feel things that a woman should not see may happen, no matter if she is a doctor" and hung up the phone.

I had seen a hatred in Prut's eyes at Grebna Baza, as I had never seen before and this had given the creeps even to me. Taking into account Prut's psychopathic coefficient, a result that I found hard to guess came out.

* * *

When I reached Place of Seven Sins in the evening, everyone was there. In turns, I greeted each of them heartily. Finally we had gathered after a very long time. The absence of some important people was clearly felt but even the gathering of the six of us was a great deal. So Lewon came to Plovdiv often. And Mehov was walking towards a humble and calm life with his wife, keeping his hands off the turbulent world.

"Fuck you, Attila! Where the hell have you been all this time? One comes around once a while", said Lewon, as he filled his glass with whiskey for the second time.

"Oh, Lewon! I wish it were as easy as said. How're you guys doing? Tell me."

"Same old, same old. Just rushing around like this."

"We're fine this way", added Mehov. Then he let off a thin whistle as he dived his middle finger downwards and lifted it up again. That was enough to liven up the laughter in all of us. An old joke...

As we lifted a toast for the sake of this, Lewon's telephone rang and he answered the phone after asking us to be a little quiet:

"Hello, my love... Yes, my love... OK, my love... We'll go to watch it in a while, my love... I didn't drink much, I'll come to pick you up, my love... OK, my love... Screw them, my love... C'mon hang up, my love..."

As we all listened smiling, Mehov couldn't wait and larked around "Well, the guy is married. You wouldn't know". Then we all drank, talked, watched the boundaries of pleasure from a distance and tried to see only the moments that we were in, as if this night was never happening. Like the ones who tried to prolong morning's sleep, we were trying to steal a few more minutes from reality, until Martin reminded us that we had arrived at the time to go.

* * *

Seven, Martin, Atanas, Lewon, Mehov and me; the six of us walked towards the entrance together. We had walked and drank all the way, and we were certified types that were there to stir up trouble. It was an illegal organization and it was quite difficult for us to get in, especially when they saw Seven and Lewon together. Martin was a thin guy and we had sent Atanas and Martin together afterwards, just so that we could get in without problem. Atanas was calmed gunpowder. Seven was a storm on the edge and Lewon an earthquake, its venous cracks visible…

All three were physically sheer giants and if the three of them looked short-tempered when together, this was just the confirmation of an already started destruction. I was able to observe after getting in with difficulty. Inside was the crowd of a night club but full of distinguished people. It was a gallery full of slobbery rich people, trying to quench their thirst for violence, and in the middle was a safeguarded ring. Every blood-thirsty rich guy's place was furnished meticulously and their high-end drinks presented to them. While hardly waiting for the minutes to pass, together with the dames who raised the bar of sexy and slutty next to them, they were letting out yells that reflected their animal impulses. While some people's lives were turned into toys, they were only concerned with enjoying it; and that had planted a separate seed of hatred inside me.

Huge bets were placed, the opening speech that fuelled the environment was given, and we started waiting for the fighters. An arse-kisser resembling a cuntface was giving the speech. We still hadn't seen Prut and in no way did they let us go to him. We were at one corner of the ring and at the other were the friends of the killers, who I wished death. We were throwing looks at each other from afar and behind each glare was enough grudge to burn even hell.

Suddenly the lights went out and all the spotlights turned to the ring. After the cuntface gave another speech, firing everyone up even more, he called Prut's opponents to the ring with flamboyant epithets. Two guys with grade three haircuts and bats in hands got into the ring. Only then did we realise that wooden bats were allowed. Obviously they wanted to guarantee the result. After the rise of an intense applause, the presenter hushed everyone with his hand and went on with his major presentation.

After the cuntface presenter made a speech that affected us too, all the lights turned to the entrance of the ring on our side. Everyone hushed and focused on the one facing death on his own. Not just curiosity, but also a fear and appreciation lay behind this silence. A muscular body walking to the light from the darkness was seen.

With the camouflage patterned trousers over the combat boots on his feet, Prut had entered under the spotlights. He was naked from the waist up. The light that hit the Stetson on his head split into two and the part that eluded the hat brought light to Prut's tattoos. He had an expression on his face, revealing that he was close to climax, and the fire of the anger in his looks brought everyone's mouth to a shush.

He walked towards his corner with slow and imposing steps. His eyes were proud and there was something different in Prut. A difference hard to see but easy to feel… I could see it only after I looked with squinting eyes. He had scraped across the winged crucifix tattoo on his chest with a knife, and a scar with a fallen scab has formed. When I looked more carefully, I saw a new tattoo right on his heart. I could see it clearly only as he walked to the middle of the ring. There was gravestone tattoo on his left chest, where his heart was, and something was written on the gravestone:

Zed

A hero was standing in the middle of the ring. A hero that would bring the piece that had fallen from the soul of our shit-show world, to peace… His head was held high and his shoulders tight. The desire of the fire of revenge in his eyes had, one-by-one, set everyone's teeth on the edge. He could have been a prophet for the sinners of a very different universe with this fire. Even his opponents greeted him hastily at the start of the fight and the symbolic referee, appointed so as not to break the cliché, extended his hand and spread the sound of the gong into the entire silence.

Prut jumped forward like a mad dog and growling, he ran to the men with his bat in his hand. The man in the front swung his bat but Prut ducked down under it and just as he was about the rise up and hit, the other one landed his kick in Prut's stomach. A psyched howl spread with one voice. This kick was strong enough to toss Prut 10-13 feet backwards.

Prut attacked as soon as he got up and the first man swung his bat again. This time Prut caught his hand holding the bat and twisted it, and knocked down the guy, who had lowered his guard, with a head butt. Even though the second man planted his right hook onto Prut's face as he turned his head, this time he remained up without jolting and he leaned sideways as the man swung the second hook, grabbing his idle arm. He had just landed three serial punches in the man's liver when the man on the ground got up and hit Prut in the calf with the bat, making him kneel. And, holding his liver, the other one kicked Prut right in the face this time. This kick had made Prut rise and fall backwards.

Insane screams rose in the gallery. Between intense cheering and swearing, Prut raised up on his fists, as if doing push-ups, lifting his head. His eyes in his blood-stained face stood like two talismans of fury. He threw a bloody spit on the floor and suddenly grabbed the bat in front of him, jumping and throwing it at the man in the front with all his strength. He had hit the guy on the head and knocked him out.

Afterwards, he lunged forward like a cannonball and running, roaring with war cries, he jumped onto the other man as if trying to crush him. He rose more than a three feet into the air and grabbed the man's head, and with a swift move, he clamped his legs around the man's waist. While serially hitting the man's head with his idle fists, on the other side he was squeezing his feet and leaving the man airless. The man could do nothing more than trying to get his head free, then Prut suddenly shouted and revealed the man's neck, pressing with his hands onto the man's head and shoulder. Then like a hunting tiger, he got his teeth into where the carotid artery was.

A shrill outcry for mercy came from the man. This shrill cry, which made everyone grimace with pity, doubled with Prut pulling back his head, and almost rang in everyone's ears. With his whole face covered in blood, Prut spit the piece of flesh in his mouth and sank his teeth in once more. Then the man was flat on the ground and blended into the silence.

After spitting the second piece of flesh in his mouth, Prut got up and went to the other man with slow steps. The man was trying to get up, holding his face, but Prut was already there before he could manage. As soon as Prut caught his collar, he threw a weak punch at Prut. This was just like cotton on steel. Prut turned his face, which had tilted to the side, and after lifting the man from his collar with both hands, he landed a strong head-butt into his face. The man's head bounced from the ground and rose about ten inches, then fell back again. Everything had developed very fast.

Prut began throwing right and left punches. Unable to slow down, he was hitting harder and harder. He hit and he hit. He hit for his pain, for the burning fury inside him. He lifted him up, hit him with his head, spat at him and starting hitting the man's head to the ground as if wanting to tear it to pieces. He went on hitting harder every time, roaring, bloody saliva gushing from his mouth. The more he hit, the more he freed himself of his shackles, and he couldn't stop. All the bones in the man's face were broken but Prut kept on beating his stiff. With his face all covered in blood, he was no different than a manslayer gone mad and he kept on hitting until the entire gallery was petrified.

He suddenly stopped and after he looked at the two dead bodies in front of him, he raised his arms to the sky, and crying "Zeeed!" he paid the redemption of his soul. Then he let his arms down and lowered his head. The silence rippled through all the looks.

The security got into the ring and took his arms but Prut began to struggle. After some scuffle, Prut took the opportunity to get free from the security, ran and jumped up, landing right on the face of the dead man who had killed Zed. God! What a disgusting sight that was! A few of the women threw up and screams rose.

The dead men's friends jumped into the ring and one of them hit Prut. I suddenly saw three angry buffalos pounce. Atanas grabbed two of them at the same time and sprung outside the ring with them. Seven grabbed the biggest one to choke him and Lewon went for the security that held Prut. Mehov also went after the security guys, following Lewon.

Martin was just starting to move, as I held his arm and said "You stand back. I don't want to become a killer too if someone hits you" and I pushed Martin backwards, heading towards someone left unattended in the ring.

The guy dodged from my first punch and landed a punch each, to my abdomen and to me cheek. I began seeing red and catching him from the throat with my left hand, I said:

"Hit me, motherfucker. Hit as hard as you can", choking him in the meantime. He was struggling but getting nowhere.

After shouting "I knead iron like dough. Who the fuck are you, you asshole", I took his head between my claws like a ball and knocked him down with a left hook. He was weaker than me. For a moment I felt sorry.

I turned my head and looked around. As Atanas was beating the two guys he had knocked down, someone came from behind and hit him on the head with a piece of wood but he couldn't get him down, and Atanas took the piece of wood from his hand and he plunged it, splintering it on the guy's head. When I looked at Seven, he had knocked out the big guy and he was holding the guy from his shoulders, hitting him on end with his own body as if smashing him into a wall. He was totally crazed and normally even he would fear himself in this state of his.

The situation was more interesting on the other side. Five bouncers were attacking Lewon and Mehov. Lewon got two of them down but the others were kicking Mehov on the floor. When one of the kicks landed real hard, it broke Mehov's thumb and the other three bouncers headed for Lewon. Lewon lost it even more when he saw the three of them. He tried to rip off his t-shirt but he couldn't because he was high; he could only get it halfway, as far as his nape. When he raised his hands and yelled like a maniac "C'mon, fuck you all. You still couldn't get me down!" the bouncers hesitated, even if there were three of them.

Just then, as I looked back, I saw someone jumping on Martin. Now that was something that shouldn't happen. I ran at them and picking up a chair, I smashed it at the guy. The chair was broken, the guy had fallen to the next table. I wanted to kill him. I was holding the broken leg of the chair and I saw that the end was sharp enough. I was just going to stab it into the guy, when a strong gun shot was heard and silence covered the place.

A crowd of security staff had surrounded us all. A man in a suit and with a gun in his hand said "You can either go home now or we'll send you someplace where there is no return". Then they ushered us outside the door.

Prut had already disappeared and this would be the last time we would see him. We all headed for Place of Seven Sins. Seven's knee was dislocated, Lewon had a black eye and Mehov's thumb was broken. We didn't talk anything that night. There was no way to start the conversation.

As Lewon grumbled "They tried a lot but they couldn't get me down, fuck 'em all", we could only smile with pain, hurting all over. That was the epilogue of the night.

* * *

I had gone up the hill in Plovdiv, where the Aliosha monument was and watched the sunrise from there. Miranda had turned into a goddess on this hill. Her last departure had been right here on a windy June evening, as was her first arrival.

I was watching Plovdiv from afar. With the pride of having witnessed all my good memories that I could live, it was silently letting the new day find life within itself. A while later a car pulled up into the car park on the hill and Seven got out. He came to me and said:

"Come with me, Attila. There is something we need to do". Then he went back to the car.

Taking me along, he drove the car to the town's exit. To the town's weary cemetery, where we buried Zed... After a 20 minute drive without a word, he parked the car in front of the cemetery. He got out, opened the trunk and taking the bottle of Flirt, Zed's bottle, he went deeper into the cemetery.

When we arrived at his grave, we noticed that it was

pretty well-kept. Obviously it was maintained a few days go and it was probably Prut who did it.

We both sat by the grave. Seven extended the bottle to me. I took one of my longest sips and handed it back to Seven. After taking a long sip himself, he got up, wet his hand from the bottle and spread it over the writing *Zed* on the tombstone.

"God rest your soul, brother. Last night Prut honoured your existence. We came here to say that. You may sleep in peace now", he said and watered Zed's grave with the bottle.

I felt an archaic tiredness in me. Seven's eyes were wet but he wouldn't let them shed. He planted the empty bottle at the top of the grave and pointed at the way out, hitting my shoulder. Maybe he was right. Maybe this visit had to be short.

I lit a cigarette and after taking two deep puffs, I bent and puffed the smoke on the writing *Zed*. I turned my back and followed Seven, leaving Zed to the void of tranquillity.

* * *

After coming back from the cemetery, we went to Place of Seven Sins and we drank until it got dark, going over our memories of the past at length. Martin had joined us later on. As we talked about each memory, having the heroes of the memory before us rendered our longings even more sincere.

The ones that burned the most were the ones including those that were no longer with us. Either ones who had forgotten this place, or ones who would never be able to come… While talking about one of these memories, Martin wanted to mention another memory related to this.

As soon as he said "Do you remember, Attila? Once you and Miranda had been…" the glass slipped from my hand and shattered to pieces. Everyone was quiet.

"I'm sorry! It just slipped out my lips. I didn't want to remind you of her", Martin said.

"It's OK, brother", I said.

As Seven got up saying "Wait, I'll get you a new one", I stopped him with my hand and said:

"No need, Seven. I wanted to get up and talk a walk around the centre anyway. Old memories made me miss the place again". I got up too and hurried myself outside.

The street lights were on and dimmed the obscurity of the night. I wanted to drink, get drunk tonight. Even if I knew I couldn't forget, I wanted to try filling the voids in the depths of my heart.

When I reached the centre, the only place I could of drinking in was Apartment 101. Since I had had enough to drink at Place of Seven Sins, I was moving mildly stumbling, my eyes blurred, but I needed more. Yesterday, Prut had been added to the ramblers who left us. Or hadn't the great disaster come to an end yet? What else could it tear away from us?

As I moved on with the tremor of this thought, Apartment 101 was already in sight. I was under the influence of alcohol, such that I felt myself more active than I was, and I was going there for more.

As I got closer, I was able to make out someone I knew standing in front of it. There was somebody waiting there and it was like I was diving more into the dream world. As I got closer, I noticed that it was a blonde woman.

Suddenly the path I walked on had turned into the gilded stones of paradise. The darkness of the night lit up with the rainbow springing from fairy tales and an intense light beam from inside the one waiting there dazzled me.

With each step, her blur first intensified, then cleared up with a distinct visuality. As I moved towards that woman in front of Apartment 101, my reality was making huge concessions. But she just looked at me, still as a statue. She never moved, said nothing.

When I got close enough to touch, I saw those ice-blue eyes. The eyes of the Goddess that looked at me, melted me inside then froze me. She was locked, watching me. I was scared. I was afraid that it was too good to be true, that she would vanish instantly.

When I stood right before her, she closed then re-opened her eyes with all her nobility. I had fallen into heaven, stood before the Goddess at an unexpected time. When I reached out my hand and held her cheek, she closed her eyes again and parted her lips. She was being liberated from her goddess-ship with a deviant sinner touching her again.

She suddenly jumped to my neck and held me tight. It was as if the warmth of her heart was burning my whole body. I held her waist. My hands were shaking and the strength in my arms was draining away. I was fighting to keep standing.

She gave me a long hug. It was at such a length that time could not measure and she said nothing. I caressed her hair. I kissed her neck and inhaled all her smell. I was totally enchanted. So much to pray that it's effect would not end…

She drew her head back and after giving life to my chapped lips with her soft lips, she set her ice-blue eyes to my weary eyes.

"Miranda!" I could only say.

After saying "I had come to find my lost rambler. And so I did", she smiled with great innocence. Then she hugged my waist and lay her head on my chest. She was the first to call us that.

Hugging her tightly, I put my hands on her golden hair, and when I raised my head to the sky, I saw the flickering stars. The moon had initiated a new musical and the stars were dancing in our honour, singing the never-ending song.

- 6 -

It was the advanced hours of the night; I had taken shelter in my house in Asenovgrad and with the minutes flowing by, step by step I was starting to believe that true peace could exist. Lying entirely naked on the corner couch in the living room, for a while I juggled the half-melted ice in the empty whiskey glass in my hand. Small pillows were placed all around me and made me feel like I was above the clouds.

What kind of a prize was this for me, who had lost even at my most deserving times? Or was it an illusion that would have to be paid for dearly later on? The only thing badgering my peace was this gnawing question. Still, I was so freshened up that this problematic was just an unseeable piece of dust.

The ice inside the empty whiskey glass kept rattling and all alone, I was watching the seeds of tranquillity playing inside the room. But like a torch running out of sources, the seeds of tranquillity were weakening. Some things were missing. The source of life that gave them vitality was missing, obviously.

When I looked at them, I saw merry kids grown tired of playing. They wanted to go on playing but they were too hungry to keep going. My eyes set upon the one at the farthest. He wanted to be included in the game but couldn't gather enough strength to make quick entrance. He was embarrassed when he noticed me watching him. He flapped his wings to make me proud and he glided through the sky, embarrassed, and let himself go into the rattling pieces of ice in the glass in my hand.

I looked into the glass. Running out of energy, he was trying to flap his wings and but in no way could he move from where he was. I wanted to reach my hand and hold him. As I reached out, a voice was heard and he darted out of the glass like an arrow. He joined his winged friends at full speed. When I looked at them, I saw that they were all focused on this energising voice.

When that voice was heard once more, saying "Attila!" they all started playing around like crazy again and with the opening of the room's door, they suddenly vanished.

Green grass reached out towards me from the doorway. Bright light filled every corner of the room and the Goddess came in with her naked body.

She was just out of the shower and every drop on her body integrated with the sparklets of lust. She posed in front of me, one hand behind her back. Then, as if drawing a weapon, she unveiled the bottle of bourbon she had hidden behind her. She had hit me in the heart with that weapon she drew. I was as hard as I could get. I was ready to kneel and worship with all my soul, but without giving me the opportunity, she came to me and kissed me from my kneecaps all the way to my chest.

Then, making a skip, she by-passed my neck and kissed my chin. She pressed her head on my chest and with her hand on the idle side of my chest, she wandered her fingers over my heart.

"I missed you so much", she said.

"I'm like a king, just back from exile."

"Then, hail the king!" Miranda said. Then she brought the bourbon bottle back to light from the place I hadn't seen her put it and brought together the whiskey in the bottle with the half-melted ice.

We let ourselves go, from the pale darkness of the night towards the insatiable lights of the dawn. Even the minute hand had given up running and surrendered itself to the arms of the hour hand. I was just curious; if the sun would be bold enough to rise.

* * *

An overcast weather with a drizzling rain, was ruling the new day. I had found the answer to my question and seen that the sun was not so bold.

For a while I watched the Goddess, her eyes closed, asleep wrapped in her innocence. Her golden hair was reaching out to surround my whole body, covering my shoulders like the unique tranquillizing waves of the ocean. In the night, belonging to our dirty worlds, we had written a mythological saga with the Goddess. We were so taken with the magic of rejoining that we ignored all that had happened and their reasons, not allowing even a hint of their existence. We never talked about old issues. We just worshipped each other, enough to make Tengri[19] angry.

The new day had begun poisoning the night's magic. The Goddess was still sleeping but she had knit her brows in her sleep and she hugged my waist tight. Obviously she was scared. She was afraid that old beauties would come together with their pain.

Taking her head under my wings, I embraced her too, like a guarding knight. I caressed her golden hair and kissed her warm temple. It had worked, Miranda had relaxed. The knit of her brows loosened and her arms, holding onto my waist as if clinging to life, swayed and started moving on my body in elliptic patterns.

She deserved a drop of peace after all we went through and there was nothing I wouldn't venture for this. I was proud, watching the innocently sleeping Goddess.

The ringing phone was what brought us back to the perception of reality.

"Hello. Good morning, Martin" I said. Miranda's ice-blue eyes opened when she heard my voice.

"Good morning, Attila. What's up?"

"Good things. Let's meet at Apartment 101 in two hours."

"OK. But don't be late. See ya."

"See ya."

After I hung the phone Miranda got up on her one arm and watched me. She was looking at me and smiling as I wandered my hands on her smooth skin. I could clearly

_____

(19)   TN: Tengri is a Turkic pagan celestial chief divinity, personifying Heaven.

see the scars of the past in her ice-blue eyes but it was too early to rake these up.

"Is Martin still here?" asked Miranda

"Yes, he is. I found out after I came back."

"Weren't you here?"

"No. I needed the roads."

"To look for me? Till you found me in London…"

"I looked a lot in the beginning but when I saw that I couldn't find you, I hit the roads. London was a miraculous coincidence. I was there to make a statue."

"I'm glad you didn't stop making statues. That has always been your antidote."

"In fact I had given up after you left. I was persuaded for just one time", I said. She paused for a moment. Then lifting her eyebrows innocently, she asked:

"Was she so beautiful? The persuader…"

"No. So alike."

She hushed and put her head back on my chest. The Goddess had started the day tiredly. After waiting that way for some minutes, I caressed her hair and said:

"Let's just let them go, everything that has stuck onto the dirty pages of the past". She held me tight, as if wanting none of them to be lived again.

"C'mon let's get up and get ready. Let's not keep Martin waiting for too long", she said.

I looked at the watch "We have 20 more minutes before we leave. Well! That's enough time", I said.

* * *

Full of beans, we had gotten out in a hurry. The 20 minute plan had doubled and probably Martin had long before arrived at Apartment 101. The car's windows were open. Miranda was smiling like a newborn baby, closing her eyes against the wind that hit her face and waved her hair.

When we reached the midpoint of Asenovgrad, we met a usual bridge traffic. As the vehicles moved slowly, I said "I wish I had taken the road below. This will slow us down quite a bit".

"It's just ten minutes to lose. That's not too much for Martin", said Miranda. Then lit a cigarette and gave it to me. Miranda didn't normally smoke but knew how much I enjoyed it.

Trying to restrain the rashness in me, waiting for the slow flowing bridge traffic, suddenly a car came from my left and dived its nose into the space in front of me. Right after him, I steered out from left and cut him off, leaning on the horn. When he honked too, I instantly pulled the parking brake and opened the car's door.

Miranda held my hand immediately. "I'll just have a chat and come back, my Goddess", I said and blew her a kiss as I got out of the car. I had no patience for fools who thought they were cunning.

When he saw me get out, the man got out too without hesitation and he was almost twice my size.

"Good! You're big enough for me not to be ashamed of knocking you down", I said as I walked towards the man.

He, too, had put his chest up with the self-confidence of his enormity and approached me, prancing. When we got very close, he looked from the top with angry looks and he shoved me, swinging his right fist, but I was at full steam. I dodged the punch and taking advantage of the space, I landed my left uppercut on his jaw. Being left-handed is a blessing on its own.

Everyone watching had probably heard the guy's teeth clashing against each other. A hiccup-like sound rose from the guy as he stumbled backwards and remained leaning on the front of his car. I spit on the man and returned to my car. Miranda was waiting indifferently, as if I was not coming back from a fight but from getting cigarettes from the shop at the corner.

"Like I said, I talked, made up and came back", I said.

"You spoke too openly", she said, as she lit a new cigarette for me. I took the cigarette from her hand and gave a small kiss.

I took a puff from the cigarette slipped into my hand and floored the accelerator. After a few asphalt-creaking wheel spinning, we darted like an arrow. We didn't talk until we got out of Asenovgrad. I don't think she cared much for my recent little dispute. Actually I didn't want to fight but things change when I'm disrespected; especially with my woman around.

* * *

We hurried up the stairs to Apartment 101. Miranda had the curious looks of an oblivious high school student, who had stepped into the headmaster's room by accident. After looking around for a very short while, Miranda was the first one to spot Martin. Martin, who didn't notice Miranda at first sight, got up when he saw us. When we got to him, we were just greeting each other and his hand froze in mid-air.

Martin had a verbal outbreak, saying "Whoa! No way!" with the silliness of surprise still upon him. "Are you kidding me?"

"If I find out it is so, I'll let you know", I answered his question.

Saying "Damned if I know!" Miranda held Martin's hand left in the air. Then she sat at one of the two empty chairs in front of Martin and waved at the young waitress for service.

"I had ordered two double vanilla vodkas for Attila and me", Martin said. "If you haven't changed your preferences, you can have that Miranda. Attila will take a bourbon and mess up my order anyway".

Miranda smiled, saying "I'll join you then. Attila will go his own way anyway", her eyes resembling pieces of eyes shiningly melting in the sun. Under obligation, I waved at the waiter or the young girl who took on that task.

"Well! Even Attila's return was something more expectable. Will one of you tell me what's happening?" asked Martin, the question I was not able to reply to yet. He folded his hand on the table like a police inspector doing an interrogation out of formality.

As he drew elliptic orbits with his thumbs, we both remained silent for a few seconds. I was the first to talk:

"Look Martin. I'm just gathering myself together from the Asenovgrad road. Why don't we go over this much later?"

"Alright, alright. In fact I don't know if I'm ready to hear it."

"Excellent."

"I'm going to slap you two ramblers", interrupted Miranda, as she sipped her vodka. "By the way, where's Zed and that Izgrev runaway?"

As Martin mumbled "Ummm… Well…" in reply, the new waitress we weren't accustomed to, brought my drink. I took a sip enough to drain half of it and said:

"They are both imprisoned in their own hells to be scorched". Martin felt an irresponsibility he didn't need.

"Attila will explain it to you better", he said, eluding the issue.

"It's better if we talk about it later", I said, without changing the dose of the sip I took from my drink. Miranda had understood that the shit had hit the fan as in the old days and talked no more. We were all silent.

Saying "Whatever you say. We'll dwell on it later", it was also Miranda who broke the silence. Sighing, she took a sip from her drink and added "C'mon let's get a bottle of beer each and go up Aliosha. Just like in the times when life was simpler…"

It was quite a reasonable offer for that moment.

Martin made a fake coughing sound to start the conversation and presented a diffidence themed excuse, saying "But Seven is waiting for me. He was talking about something crazy like doing a master's degree at this age. The interesting part is that he wants to enlist me too".

"OK, OK. I'll drop you off at Seven's on the way", I said. On one hand, this had become a nice opportunity to end the day that we had half-started with Miranda.

* * *

The sun's dimming hours were harassing each other and the one beer issue was just a lie. Partially, at least… Taking into account the two-litre beer bottles in Bulgaria, I couldn't even count how many bottles we sent down Aliosha's cliff.

Damn! We were on a side of the Aliosha hill which I couldn't exactly guess and this was exactly the place where Miranda and I had started to belong to each other.

All the dreams, which I built simple enough to become true, so that they would become true, were becoming true. And then some… Still, a heavy bends of worry was still preying on me inwardly. Was it my dreams, which I had reduced to simpler than ordinary so that they would be realized, watering this seed of worry; or was I caught in the probability of these dreams, which were successful for the first time, definitely coming with their infortunium?

Miranda's hand, throwing my hair back and caressing my cheek, pulled me back. I smiled, looking at her face. I had missed these vital savings of Miranda and now, with great zest, she was giving life to the only reality that I took pleasure in accepting.

"You haven't changed a bit, have you? You are still the Attila, who I can read like an open book", said Miranda, as we sipped our decreasing beer stock. Her face was turned to the wind that blew her hair back and she never looked at me.

"Well! You know my favourite saying", I said.

"Sure: People don't change. Time passes by and they just forget who they are."

"Absolutely!"

"Fine but what if we are imprisoned in a time where we forget who we are and refuse to change, to return to our old state?" she asked.

There you go! My woman... The only person who knew my weakest points was again hitting me with one of my weakest points. Actually this made me feel good. It proved that I was not the only person drowning in his own shit, that I had a one in a billion knower. The only person enabling me to elude loneliness... Had the current world population gone over six billion? I need to know the estimated number.

I took sips from the beer, long enough to test the length of my breath holding, and turning to Miranda, I answered her question "On our first day right here, I vowed that I would forever be the way you first found me, Miranda. Even if you relent this, Tengri would try me with Tamu[20]. Sky in, red out!"

The same fervour, which I felt after taking the sledge-hammer in my hand after a long time, had filled into my veins. I hadn't even realized how I tossed the half-full beer bottle in my hand down the cliff.

Miranda took out the packet of cigarettes from the pocket of my jacket, which she had put on her right side, and took one out, lit it and handed it to me. I took it from her hand and fanned it with a few strong puffs. Then, feeling my eyes suddenly starting to flicker, I let the half cindered cigarette fly down the cliff after the beer bottle.

I mumbled "Optimistic drama!" as I grasped the

---

(20)   TN: Tamu is an ancient Turkish word for hell.

packet of Davidoff from Miranda's hand and lit a new one from it.

* * *

Ever since the first moment we met, we were not dwelling on anything too much. Without deepening issues too much, we returned home to make the moments that we had been longing for a long time, pieces of our lives again. In fact a totally irrelevant parasite was almost complicating our path. Thank God, I had offended her courage so much that she couldn't build it up against me again.

After coming down from Aliosha, moving towards the car I had left close to the park in the centre, a familiar trotting body had appeared at the end of the street leading to the tunnel.

When I carelessly got too close than necessary, I first came across a set of full breasts, then Valeria's slutty looks, and this on its own, was like the messenger of the nausea I didn't even want to dream of.

Luckily, maybe for the first time that I would appreciate her manners, Valeria went on her way after taking a short glance, as if she had looked unwillingly.

We passed by each other so close that our shoulders almost rubbed against each other. After a few steps Miranda, still holding my arms, grumbled:

"Eww… She gave me the creeps. Attractive, yet repulsive to the same degree."

"Who?"

"I'm talking about the slutty one that just passed us by."

"You're talking to me about people?"

"OK. Never mind", said Miranda, as she put her head on the shoulder of my arm she had her hand around. There was no expression on her face. She just absently watched the road in front of us, her resting head moving with our steps.

* * *

I met Miranda's smile when I opened my eyes with a poke. After she got me up, I went to the living room and saw that our morning coffees were already prepared. An ideal tranquilliser for a morning starting lazily...

As I had begun to enjoy the coffee with a smoke, my eyes stretched towards the ventilator blowing from below, the doorbell rang. This was a harassment occurring earlier than expected for such a calm morning.

When I opened the door, I saw Atanas and Teodora with their smiling faces.

"It's us, Mr. Attila", said Atanas.

"Friends of the family, welcome!"

"We came unannounced but you're available, right?" asked Teodora.

As I invited them in, saying "What kind of a question is that? Come on in, don't wait", first Martin then Seven came in after them. Before I had to ask, Martin enlightened me:

"C'mon get ready. We're going to Bachkovo, to nature. Orders of the manager!"

Without wasting much time, we got ready and set on the quarter-hour drive, and the weather was ideal for this plan. The place consisted of a historic monastery at the edge of the hill. Climbing up the hill, there was a place usually preferred by picnickers and when you weren't lazy and climbed up further, you could reach the second area, where not too many people visited, which harboured a creek, grass, trees, a hill and everything else that could be in a portrait of nature. We were among those who weren't lazy and enjoyed the lonely pleasure of the place.

With me looting my last remaining alcohol stash before leaving the house, we had an ample stock of booze. After getting some more extras on the way, we reached Bachkovo. Without fooling around, after a mountain walk that lasted over half an hour with pauses, we reached our destination and to start with, we buried the booze in the cold creek. Then we layed down onto the green.

"Attila, will we able to finish this much alcohol? I don't intend to carry them back", said Seven, with one hand on his nape and the other taking the bottle to his mouth.

"I dunno. We have enough time so see that", I answered, smiling. He extended his bottle and clinked it to mine, and we both took our sips. Seven laid his bottle on the grass and said:

"The issue of seeing the bottom of the bottle began to remind me Zed too often nowadays."

I could just say "Apparently it will go on that way from now on". We both shared the same feeling and we watched the view silently for a while, continuing to sip our drinks. There was a very vivid view. The sun was making everything that nature embraced shine. It was very inspiring, with its clarity that proved my eyes still worked. So, I'm talking about true, pure inspiration. Much further than a poet's erection that is enchanted by every fiddle-faddle. The only oar that the ones, who find their purpose in life, use in this struggle…

"Hey Seven look. Are you going to spice these meat? You're good at it", called Atanas, as he fanned the flames he had lit.

Seven prepared the meat with Atanas and put them on fire. Together with the girls, Martin was fiddling with the bags they had brought. Feeling the nature deeply, I went to the creek and replaced the bottle in my hand with a random colder one. Then, after watching the bottles that the creek washed over, I took an extra bottle with me and went by the fire.

With Seven's touch, the meats were being grilled so nice that it made our mouths water. I extended the other bottle in my hand to Atanas and asked "The appetisers are great but do you think we can consume all this booze?"

"Take it easy, Attila. Teodora prepared a tea from her rare herbs, with a recipe full of secrets", he answered, winking, as he continued to fan the flames.

"So? What use will the tea be?"

"Don't say that. It is a booze recipe. It adds much more quality to the drunkenness of the booze", he said and added "And also very relaxing for the stomach", looking at Seven. Seven's stomach problems sometimes could really turn into nightmares for him while drinking.

A grateful smile covered Seven's face. "Ah! Good then. Pour me some right away. I trust you doctors", he said. First Seven, then everyone else got their teas. In a short while, the tea began to show its effects significantly. Afterwards, with the relaxation it brought, sipping drinks with this tea became the day's indispensable.

When the appetisers were prepared, the effects of alcohol had already enwrapped our bodies. Frankly, it was an overly interesting tea. Although I stopped the booze and drank only tea for a while, my fuddle grew stronger instead of being reduced. I guessed that there were some heady herbs in it too. Still, there is no sense in questioning it so much. How dangerous can a doctor's recipe be?

After about half an hour more passed, we all found ourselves lying on the grass, taking advantage of the earth that gave it life. Seven suddenly straightened up and said "I felt very relaxed. Now it's time for a nice smoke" and after fumbling with the bags a bit, he brought out a tobacco case full of high quality Bulgarian tobacco. As he rolled up a cigarette without wasting any time, Martin got up the same way and asked:

"Hey! Did you bring that tobacco from Kardzhali?"

"I won't say where I found it. If you stop smuggling Raki and look around a little, you can find some yourself too", replied Seven, as he continued to roll his cigarette. After rolling the cigarette he handed it to Martin. Martin, after taking this ordinary looking cigarette and looking at it from different angles like examining a Cuban cigar, said:

"OK but you mucked rolling up this thing. You really messed it up. Give it to me, I'll roll one and show you how it's done", and after fiddling with it for a while, he showed us the cigarettish thing, double the size of Seven's. After saying his final words "Besides, mine is big enough for everyone", he handed it to Seven. Seven lit it with the expertise of an oenologist examining a fine wine and passed it to the crowd. Curling his lips and raising his eyebrows, he approved Martin's rolling ability with a positive mimic rarely expected from him. Like kids trespassing in a candy store, we were passing the twist to each other in turns and with curiosity, when Martin unexpectedly lit the second twist and passed it on from the opposite direction.

While passing each other the hand rolled cigarettes one from the right and the other from the left, they both turned and concurred at Miranda. Martin raised the bottle in his hand and enthusiastically yelled "Estarabim!"[21] upon this. Half of us could only listen to him with curious looks, devoid of meaning.

Miranda first looked at the twists in both of her hands. Then, as if taking a sip from her drink, she took one puff from each. Everyone was curiously watching Miranda's reaction, and when she too, like Seven, curled her lips and raised her eyebrows and said:

"Mmm… It's really good, Martin. In fact, it was one of the best twists I've had. Maybe you should give it a name. Like; Martinoff!" suddenly everyone, including herself, burst with laughter. It seemed that an alcohol-patterned stramash had begun.

The hours passed by, just as they had started. Everyone's joy had grown step by step. While plentily reminiscing old days, we had gone seriously deeper into issues

(21)   TN: Estarabim is a term invented by Turkish musician Erkin Koray. It means in a puff puff pass circle where two joints exist, a person happens to come across with both of the joints coming from each side.

related to this. We really liked scrutinising things worth dwelling on. Actually I had poked into a few matters more than necessary and gotten into oval-ended polemics with Seven. We laughed at it afterwards and we suddenly settled down and stopped the chat.

It was the tiredness of a satisfied conversation of a drunken crowd. Taking advantage of the opportunity arising from silence, we buried ourselves into our drinks and hurriedly tasted all the appetizers one by one. Then we threw the blanket on the ground aside and let ourselves go on the grass that we tried to feel, and that was mildly moistened with the spilling booze.

I had put my head on the extended legs of Miranda, who had leaned on a tree that created half a shadow, and there was less than 15 feet between us and the crowd.

They heard everything we said but didn't even care of what they themselves said. I looked into the sky. Everyone was watching an element of nature without making much of a sound. An unconscious rite, which threw into the trash all our accumulations outside the area that we could see, dominated the minutes.

Miranda caressed my head for a while. I could feel the tingling on my forehead and, in a fitting manner, the pale sky was inside a meaningful tedium. I thought of the past and leaped into the past of all the individuals that sunk into my being. I thought of my mother and father. And of course, of my two cousins with whom I came here for the first time…

I guess the path, in which my parents' life fell into, was going stable as per my expectations. The thing that mildly attempted to harass my curiosity was the condition of my cousins. I had grown up with the two of them until I was of lawful age. The last thing I remember was that the elder one was a professional merchant and the smaller one was a standard family man, a long while ago.

As I looked away, being disturbed by the sun spitting directly into my eyes, I saw smiles flowering in everyone's faces. This epidemic had spread with the silence that grew stronger after the elapsed hours. Without dilatory, I could say hello to a judgement that was carelessly born after a short ceremony of curiosity: Dreams were simpler and turmoils were greater. Or was it not so, as we each danced in the surreality of the scenery we got lost in? At least the smiles, standing contented against the wind, made it clear that either one of the dreams or the turmoils were reduced to a minimum. Apparently, the only place this smile fell short was Miranda's face and mine.

I was suddenly startled with a few drops of liquid splashing on my face. When I looked up at the place, right above my head, where the liquid was spilling from, Miranda wet her hand with my bourbon bottle and splattered my face again.

"Heyyy! Come back to the world we are condemned to", she said and wandered her still wet hand over my face like applying cream.

I stuck out my tongue and licked the remaining wetness on my lower lip. "If it were somebody else, I would have started a blood feud for torturing my drink like that", I said and with a wrestler's move, I got Miranda under me.

As soon as I brought her wrists to the touché position, she started laughing and kissed my close-for-contact lips. I decreased the force I was applying on her wrists.

Involuntarily, taking advantage of this, she freed her hands and embraced my head, giving life to a passionate kiss that climaxed in a few seconds. As soon as I became incapable with this suddenly climaxing display, Miranda made her real move and swung me and got back on top. The Goddess did not look frail, and was strong too. But I had the ability to control my adrenalin, a gift acquired next to forging iron, and as Miranda kept smiling on top of me, I clasped her waist and got her back under me with a single move, like a predator making contact with its prey.

Along with the increasing adrenalin, my testosterone involuntarily gave similar reaction and I started kissing Miranda's neck. Just as I was including my hands in the game, a "Whoa, whoa!" sound neutralized the whole action. Martin, extending both arms to the sides, smilingly reproved "We're here too. Be a little more patient to go home". Just like the old cablecasts blurring after a certain hour, the spell had broken at the most crucial moment.

So I went to the creek with a smile and replaced the bourbon with another cold one, took Miranda's favourite vanilla vodka as extra and put my head back onto the legs of Miranda, who was resting her back on the tree. Miranda was still smiling. The normal one was fine, but her smile really full of pure sincerity was something I could rarely witness, like the eclipse of the Sun.

Miranda was watching the mountains far away and I was watching Miranda. She caressed my hair for a while, without looking at me, and then turning her eyes to me she asked:

"How is your Bulgarian? Is there any improvement or recline?"

"Depends on the situation."

"How?"

"If it suits me, I let it flow. Otherwise I'm bloody illiterate."

"Let's test it then", she said and started to look around. As she wandered her looks around the close surroundings, she noticed a bee coming at her and suddenly let out a short cry. She was allergic to bee sting. I did my job and shooed off the bee immediately.

"Tell me now, what is Bulgarian for bee?" she asked without waiting and without thinking about it.

"Hmm…Бубулечка!" I replied, sure of myself.

"No, that doesn't count. What you said means bug."

After saying "I see", I thought for a few seconds but nothing came to my mind and everyone, with their high heads, were focused on my answer. I looked around for a while and when I replied "Then; flying Бубулечка!" with an even greater self-confidence, everyone burst out into loud laughter.

After fooling around in Bachkovo a while more and exhausted the overtime hours, at one time I turned my looks back at the sky again. The clouds who slapped the sun away to the hole it belongs, clearly indicated that it was time for us to go. We packed in a short time and headed back.

* * *

By the time I was able to open my eyes, the time was already pressing on nightfall. Miranda was still sleeping. We could only sleep with the new day dawning, after a long and exhausting sex that activated all my sweat glands. For the first time, after a period so long that I could not remember, I had woken Miranda. This was rare event, occurring only at times when she had more to drink than I. Probably because of the vanilla vodka.

There was quandary in the Goddess' breathing of the new day. Even if I was able to easily guess it with a mild push, this attitude of Miranda was one of the numbered representatives that could sincerely frighten me. In fact, it was the seed of deadwood that, until now, were never able to assume the adjective of being good. I didn't know anything but I was undoubtedly hearing once more the sounds of the crack, which had turned into a bottomless pit before, based on fake innocence.

Even though I saw the single drop of poison that had probably long before fallen on the Goddess' soul, I did something unbecoming for any gentleman, even for a rambler. It was a move, found obscene by masturbation addicts who have never even laid hands on a prostitute, to start satisfying my morning.... rather, my evening erection.

She did not oppose, nor did she talk. Even if she never refrained from our lust even under tough conditions, she also never failed to show the colour of her mood clearly and make the job difficult at the same rate. In fact, that was what bloated up the suspicion in me. The only strike falling on the silence were the gradually increasing moans. She could only utter her first words only after my hormonal pressure got back to normal values:

"C'mon let's go to Bezisten and have something to drink", she said, leaning her head on my chest with her eyes open. For a while I caressed her golden hair, running my fingers around them. Even if I couldn't remember the last time we went there together, it was the times when we drowned in the hallucination of happiness. Right then, I accepted that the poison I saw falling into her was the final straw and that we had hooked on the time to face the reality that we were trying not to put into words since the first day we met. Without fooling around, we headed for Bezisten.

* * *

Bezisten was its usual self, presenting its sincere companionship only to the ones who could put up with its gloom. Miranda and I were exceptions, risen to the status of old friends.

We got the stools and settled at where the bar met the wall. Miranda was on my right and on her right was the wall. She had consciously settled at my right knowing that, as a lefty smeared with paranoia, I always tried to keep my left side open and alert.

A small-breasted but beautiful barmaid came across us. I felt sympathy, involuntarily, because she smiled heartily, rather than because of the job. Just behind her was the regular fixture barmen, who looked a lot like a Mel Gibson with long hair. The girl was new but Mel Gibson's reflection was giving the years a run for their money. He was the one who gave me my beer on the first day I came here and now years later, probably he would be the one to prepare my bourbon.

He couldn't make me out from a distance but after squinting his eyes for a few seconds and checking me out, he recognized and lifted his thumb, making a sign of approval.

I greeted him shouting "Hey, Braveheart!" in his own language and saluted him from afar. Even though I had seen him for a period long enough to almost knock down a generation, I never asked his name and neither did he ask mine… I had made it a habit calling him Braveheart. And he had accepted this, never took offense probably because of me being a stranger. Maybe one day when I'm not lazy, I'll ask his name.

When the barmaid asked "Yes, what would you like?" I smoothly turned my eyes towards Miranda.

Saying "The best bourbon in the bar and vanilla vodka. Make them both double. And also two shots from the first bottle you get your hands on", she clearly specified our orders.

The barmaid must have missed the last part so she asked "Shot of what?"

Without dealing with the subject so much, Miranda replied "The first one you get your hands on, I said. If that's too complicated, make it your favourite one", with the hint of a mild reproach.

As soon as the barmaid turned around to prepare the orders, Miranda took two cigarettes from the box of Davidoffs I had just taken out of my pocket and lit them both, handing me one. As she smoked the other cigarette,

I could hear the sounds of the closing storm very clearly now. As I could remember without difficulty, Miranda had had her last smoke, other than lighting it for me, in the second month of our relationship and then had quit it with a sudden decision. Now she was smoking no different than a locomotive funnel.

"I didn't want a shot", I said, dropping the ash of my cigarette on the ground without letting the barman see.

"I know. That's why I asked for only two for myself", replied Miranda. And then we went on silently puffing on our cigarettes until our drinks arrived.

Miranda was talking with an elite and clean Bulgarian that even most Bulgarians couldn't acquire. Until I had barely memorized her past, I had thought she was a sheer Bulgarian during our entire first year. But it is not possible for a Goddess, who can make the whole world tremble, to be born from a single mythology, right?

Once upon a time she had told me about her racial formation; in a past, which is still in my memory but which I fear to remember because it will once again bleed my wound, encrusted down deep. That bastard thought I struggled with for years was the first drop of water falling onto my fire, as I worshipped her tiniest sparklet. It was a race that insulted Tengri, one of the races that flowed in Miranda's veins. The days I really got to know Miranda, were the days I challenged Tengri. Maybe that is why I am burning in the fiery flames of Tamu for the last few years that I haven't been able to keep count of.

When the barman brought our drinks after a few minutes, he saw the cigarettes in our hands and coolly said "Excuse me, you are not allowed to smoke indoors", as per his duty.

Miranda looked around the bar a bit without reacting, and after she saw the no smoking sign, she squinted her eyes and thought for a short while. Then she put money onto the bar, enough for our smoking penalties, our drinks and a generous tip for the barman.

As the barman said nothing, put an ashtray in front of us and turned around, Miranda had already sloshed down the second shot glass. I spinned the glass in front of me two turns and took a large sip, emptying half of it. And Miranda put out the cigarette, whose half looked like a rocket from puffing so quickly, in the ashtray and put her hand on my right leg after taking a short sip from her drink.

When I turned my gaze upon her, she had already fixed her ice-blue eyes on me. She had bent her head slightly and opened her eyes fully, giving me the erotic looks that I could not resist. She had slightly parted her lips as if she was going to say something. A slightly bent neck, eyes fixed on me and half-open lips… Miranda knew very well the key that stimulated my libido. Of course I don't know if this is also true for anyone else. Which move of the Goddess wouldn't effect a sinning worshipper?

"Watch out, you're igniting it", I said, but absently in Russian. With a punch landing on my abdominal cavity, lightning striked and the ambience changed abruptly. She did not like Russian or anything about the Russians, getting angry at once when she heard it. In the past I rarely used to add Russian words to my talk, just to make her angry for fun. She didn't tell me the reason for all this time and I, feeling no need for probing, attributed it to jealousy and brushed it over in my own way.

Yes, Miranda was jealous. And plenty at that. Even during the times we had first met, she had masterfully cursed at all my girlfriends she met. Her choice of words were not swearing unreservedly, but words chosen carefully, striking the right note. I had instantly noticed her ability to use words. There were also times of verbal diarrhoea that we had when we were alone with each other. Times of twaddle. Maybe this part had the most active role in impressing one another. Even when we rambled about quite irrelevant words and seriously increased the level of bullshit, we could surpass the things told, which everyone else got stuck on, and guess which mood the other one of us was floating in, and enjoy for hours the assuming these two moods into one body.

"I can't take it anymore, Attila", said Miranda, as she extended her hand towards the glass rather hesitantly. "All that's happened… Thinking about these… Doesn't ease off in time. On the contrary, it irritates me inside more every day, growing like a snowball. In the beginning it seemed to be going fine after getting away from everything. In time, everything had become as blurry as a nice dream and a creepy nightmare, which I see both in the same sleep. In fact, even if forced some more, I even could have believed that it wasn't real, but this life is not that magical. First your silhouette hitting my mind like a slap in London and now your presence next to me in flesh and blood… There is no escape after what happened. Every escape is just a surreal deviation, only until returning to the path you belong".

After releasing her venom without interruption, she took a deep breath, squinted her eyes and dropped her shoulders and her head. The Goddess was tired. No words could leave my mouth. Since Miranda was four inches taller than me, I took her head under my wings by moving her close to me, having to pull her stool, and all I could do was to hold her as if proving that I would never leave her alone.

Standing with Miranda in my arms, our memories from our first day till today began to visualise before my eyes. She was fearful and weak when I found her. Only her rebel soul, which made her blood boil, instilled resolution to her. With the pain of her father, whom she had lost half a year before we met, she was living life without a goal, just because it had to be lived.

When I first held her hand, we both rebelled at the tomorrows. I had accepted it as my duty and worked a lot to strengthen her as much as possible. We fluttered together in life's impositions, which other people saw fit. Even if she had qualities that fell contradicted with most of my convictions, she almost depictured my real frailties.

We had matured together with the passing of years that would each bludgeon a separate average life. In fact, to be honest, she was the one who matured me. I was living life with a childish rage, until she became a part of it. She was again the one who watched for the existence of the good structures, which I was ready to immediately set to flames with the fire inside me, by re-enforcing their basis. In time she also showed me how to do this and then together we began to build the unique temples that we hoped would stretch to eternity.

Minutes, months, days, weeks and breath-taking moments… With our passions that had hooked on every concept that separated from within the concept of time, we believed that we could crush everything that dared to challenge us like insects, until we lost control of the steering wheel. That night, I hadn't just lost the control of the car but also of the joyful desire that gave my life direction.

While the vehicle coming from the opposite direction was trying to overtake the one in front of it, showing his indexterity and not being able to either overtake or get back to his lane again, he tried to swing his car out of my side of the road, and not managing that either, he crashed head on from the side Miranda was sitting.

Until Miranda got out of the coma in the hospital, with my unproportional paranoia, all bad scenarios had each taken two turns inside my head. I had heaved a sigh of relief with the doctor saying that everyone was in good health, but only for an annoyingly short while.

She was two months pregnant and with this accident Miranda had had a miscarriage. With the fragmented pieces of the car that stuck into her womb during the accident, together with the unborn baby she had also lost her ability to give birth again.

When I asked why she hadn't told me, she had explained that she feared me running away because I didn't want a child. At that time I was at the top parts of my career and when we had talked about a child earlier, I had said that I was absolutely not ready for this. She had consented to carefully hide what she resented, not to lose me. In fact, she wanted me to make her my suitcase if one day I should decide to leave.

It seemed like an issue that could be gotten over, even if it was difficult, but there was one point I had ruled out: The fact that Miranda could never be a mother again. The consequence that horrified her deeply and even razed her to the ground, was this one. She had forever lost this natural feature that she feared even to talk about so as not to destroy my life, and moreover, in an accident I had made.

Everything began to get worse in time. Even though she got the creeps over getting attached, she wanted to be a family. Our habits, thoughts, choices, clothes, reactions and way of perception… Almost everything about us was in a dissimilarity opposing society. She didn't want to be a freak anymore; wanted to live like simple people did. She envied the normal, as she watched the lives we fluttered in. I, on the other hand, was busy trying to explain that all we had were blessings given to us and that a talisman that could turn us into an immortal legend lay in her heart. After a period, too short to have the chance of building a balance, she could no longer bear the heavy load on her soul and left without a trace on one vituperative June morning.

Somehow a spell had come true and brought the Goddess, who right now took refuge under my wings for some compassion, back to me. I caressed her hair some more and gazed over the bottles in the bar, then taking a few deep and long breaths, I could only ask:

"Everything was going so well, ah, were it not for those

feelings! Or was happiness the forbidden apple that we shouldn't eat, Miranda?" without waiting for an answer. The callus on my hands drew a rough path, getting caught in the golden hair.

"What more is left to fill the purpose of life, if not feelings?" she asked. Maybe she was right.

"Since you left, I don't quite have memories that can plant seeds into my feelings. Yet, I go on living. At least I think so."

"I don't think so", said Miranda immediately, undermining my words.

"Then what do I have to gain in this?"

"We have our freedom. The only fact that could make you give up on feelings, I guess."

"Freedom? Freedom is having the morning smoke with whiskey instead of coffee." I said.

"Absolutely. But it is something to possess it and something else to rule it", she added. Every word we used tired me. I lifted her head, planted a soft kiss on her lips, one that would be pleasant to feel, and took her under my wings again. This kiss had hurt us both inside. I felt the fever in my eyes.

"You know the most hurtful part is, rather than everything else? I one by one began to forget all the beautiful memories that I had once rendered indispensable", I said, squinting my eyes so as to imprison my tears. I didn't want her to see this sight.

She suddenly buried her head in my shoulder and held my arm with both hands. I heard a few sobs and she began to squeeze my arm with all her might. She was hurting. When I lifted her head and looked at her face, I saw ice-blue eyes turned into bloodshots with crying. My hands began to shake. I was having a hard time bearing to see her teardrops. After taking a few breaths drowning in sobs, she sloshed down all the drinks in front of us one by one and gave me the roughest kiss of my life. Both of our lips were torn and blood filled our mouths.

Her tears became intensified and after a "Forgive me!" wish coming out between her bloody lips, she left the bar running as fast as she could. When I looked after her, all I could see was the transparent darkness of the night.

- 7 -

All night I looked for Miranda non-stop. I had looked into every corner of Plovdiv several times, stepping on the gas pedal hard enough to smash it. The fact that I could find no trace despite this, only paid share to the suspicion in me to unlimitedly intensify.

As cold sweat, partial to panic attack, covered my whole body, I was thinking of places I might have missed and trying to console myself with the idea that Miranda could be there. It was an empty and silent Plovdiv night. Quite empty... Deep emptiness...

After an aimless hunt that went on for hours, an unknown number rang my phone close to dawn. The spear Tengri threw, destroyed my entire being. It was the police calling. They had found Miranda's lifeless body, with slashed wrists, at the bottom of Aliosha Hill, and called me to the hospital for identification. Two deep cuts on her left wrist. One for her and one for me...

* * *

I hit everything that my eyes could see; walls, rocks, cars on the road, traffic sign boards, bus stops and every metal structure. I hit all the high-resistant material. Until it came down, or I did…

The sun had risen red. Only terror and blood reigned my pupils. The phenomenon of grudge that I felt for the first time in my life was cracking, to the death, the veins embosomed all the way to the furthest points of my body.

I wanted to destroy the world and all that it harboured within. I wanted to tear it to its molecules, in the real sense, like an exploding star. A godlike power is necessary for this. Yes, God…

I could only murmur "Oh Tengri! If you really exist, bring along the doomsday that everyone fears. If you don't exist, then we have already seen the worst of it. But if you are there and can't dare doomsday, then give me your powers. I'll show you how to be a proper god. I openly challenge you. Come, if you are man enough. You must be male, because the Goddess is dead", left breathless.

* * *

When we reached the cemetery, the sun was right at the top. We weren't a crowd. Besides the seedy ramblers, there were only two very old friends of Miranda. Even though Miranda's half-brother, who was a priest, wanted to come, I didn't allow him to be there, knowing that Miranda would never forgive him for what he had done.

The numbered people there were as if in a great shock. I could read this in their eyes. I thought of all that had happened, just taken place in this month alone.

Because I hadn't fully learned Miranda's system of belief, we all presented her an honourable farewell in our own ways. After the part of the ceremony full of prayers passed, I dug the dry soil with my own hands. The earth had hardened, as if rejecting to take the Goddess. It was ashamed. I had ashamed even the dry earth torrid in the midday heat. I had even challenged Tengri for this cause but there was still no sound from him.

I didn't want to talk. I couldn't dare to talk. The poison inside me was always ready to stain my words. My left hand began shaking again. As we were placing the casket screwed with red-painted metals into the hole in the dry earth, I was even avoiding to notice the legendaryness of the moments bearing a great farewell. When I took the shovel back into my hands to cover the casket after placing it, the dose of the shaking in my left hand increased even more.

I was still not ready for this ceremony but it had to happen. The minutes engraving into the hour were by my side and they resisted to flow, even if it included an impossibility. What was happening now couldn't be real. It shouldn't. After swinging the shovel embracing the final piece of soil, we carried out the last part of the ceremony and I let our ramblers go, to water Zed's grave. Miranda had also taken her place in the cemetery where her father and Zed tried to sleep in peace.

* * *

Seven called me in the evening hours.
He could only say "Hello, Attila. I know what you're

going to do. Come to me before the last good-bye. Your place at the bar is ready".

With spinning the wheels, so much that they would have to be replaced, I burst out of where I was and headed for Place of Seven Sins. As I got there in a short while, I knocked on the door and Seven immediately started saying:

"I don't know where to right now, but I know that you will be leaving again very soon", as soon as he opened it.

"Are you about what you're saying?"

"Absolutely! Or course if the Attila I've always known hasn't changed…"

Oh Seven, if only every woman I met before meeting the Goddess again could catch even a smallest part of your mentality. If they really did exist, even horny Adam and pervert Eve would be slaves to this path we thought-lessly started walking.

"Look, Attila. I'm not a child. I know that you'll be hitting the roads again and that this time there will be no coming back."

"Don't be so sure."

"Attila!" he said, quite emphatically.

"OK, I'll keep quiet. Still, foresight is a dirty gift, which we actually don't want to have, Seven."

"Even the most lettered ones can't guess what tomor-row will load. Just set your next move carefully."

"Who cares?"

"You do!" he said, hardening his tone even more and then he gave permission to a few seconds of silence, and took three calm sips from the beer he had just opened.

"Seven, I don't feel so well. I need to get home and

170

spare some time from myself. Besides, I have some paperwork to be embarked on tomorrow", I said as I got up.

"OK. No need for a lot of explanation, I know."

"Somehow I always feel a debt for explanation to you", I said, bitterly trying to smile. When I turned around and looked into Place of Seven Sins one more time as I was getting out the door, I saw Seven trying to place the half-full bottle of Jim Beam, which he had poured into my glass a while ago, at the upper parts of the bar.

* * *

As I was trying to take anything, which could try to be useful, from the artificiality of the fictions that scratched my mind, I was covered in reality again with my kick that broke the door of my house. I didn't know exactly what to do in accordance with logic, so I could only target the turbidity that served my spiritual reality.

Each of the kicks I had started with the entrance door had perfectly grovelled to their non-essential targets and tasted every simple disaster that submitted to mankind. I didn't want to get involved in the prejudicial innocence. So, I even threw my own convictions into the trash, just so that the strikes would meet their right tones.

A few minutes ago I spit at the table clock that was past twelve in the night and together with the bottle of bourbon that I just got halfway through, I dashed out of the house, taking the car keys. With the dangerous drive alcohol offered me, I had reached the cemetery in the fastest way possible.

After watering the crabgrass in leaf on Zed's grave with

a quarter of the half-full bottle, I sloshed the remaining quarter down as if it were water and came in front of Miranda's father's grave, thanked him for playing a part in bringing such an adorable Goddess into the world. This creator had died because of drugs he had taken together with alcohol. Creator of the Goddess… After presenting my thanks, even though I had never met him, I directed my steps towards the Goddess' eternal sanctuary. Every step of mine, wearied my legs even further.

In no way could I make out what I would do. Although my breath was agonized, yesterday I thought I had dug my claws into the world's heart with all their anger, until proved otherwise. But the Goddess had blended into the heart of the fertile earth and there was only God left before me that I could face. Until the first day of my new life after today, which had started yesterday, I had really believed that mercy could truly exist. I had tried to curse Tengri as much as he had damned me and since he still hadn't answered, I can officially assume that I was successful at this.

My steps exhausted the last of their energy when I reached before the Goddess' sanctuary. I raised my shoulders and looked around. It was a dry and gloomy night. In the area as far as my eyes could see, there was nothing else than hundreds of dead lying around. I was not feeling out of it. Maybe now I too, belong right here.

It was a one-sided contract imposed by fate: The innocent girl dies and the arsehole rambler lives.

Inside of me, deep down, I felt a stratified warmth. Suddenly flaring up, it first bent my left knee, then the right. It had made me kneel before the Goddess' shrine and suddenly its twinges become ten times more frequent like a fastened nightmare. The sleeping volcano became active and started to climb up my throat with its sharpest kindle. Frying me inside gradually with every inch, it reached the final point.

When its burn finally wrapped around my tongue, I grasped the dirt on the ground with its eye-watering pain. After fighting back with all my might for a few seconds, I could take it no more and surrendered.

My screams resounding the cemetery started slapping the darkness of the night. My flaming cries were shattering all my existing emotions, filling the dirt in my palms with stained mourning. I wanted to perish. To spite everything that couldn't destroy me until now, I wished to perish. As my non-stop cry came close to exhausting all of my strength, I managed to stop my cry with the final few drops remaining from it, and raised my head to the sky.

"Hey Tengri! This is my last call for you. Prove!" was all I could yell and with my zapped out strength, my eyes closed and my head fell.

My strength had zeroed, my breath heavy. I needed a proof. A way out… I was rejecting to open my eyes with my hopelessness that prayed for all of this to be untrue. C'mon Attila! A little courage! There was nothing left anyway.

I starting parting my eyes slowly. There was still nothing more than the dirt in my hands. When I opened my eyes completely, I looked at the dirt in my palms again and at that moment something caught my eye. There was a tiny piece of paper stuck inside the mound of dirt in my left palm. The writings on it were long erased but just then a lightning struck my mind.

I got up coughing and got into my car, heading for the empty piece of land in the backyard of the building where Martin lived.

* * *

When I was halfway there, a warm rain that mildly drizzled, as if dripping, had begun. I parked the car in front of the building block where Martin lived and went to the back side from the pathway next to the building, without Martin knowing at all. When I looked from the empty land at the back of the building, the lights on Martin's floor were lit. This non-informing of mine will piss him off a lot.

I needed a definite answer. I was either going to run or go deeply insane. Maybe suicide. When I look at the state I am in now, with my hunger for this answer, I can even hook onto the piece of hope at the farthest corner.

In the middle of the empty land, I began looking around in the dark. Objects could hardly be made out in the darkness. After looking around for ten minutes, I had begun to think that I was living in a dream world full of fantasies, when I saw pieces of broken glass on the ground. Pieces of broken wineglass…

As I bent down and pulled the pieces of glass, I met a footmark of a heeled shoe pressed hard, and God once more proved his existence. I began digging the footmark with bare hands. The drizzling of the warm rain was softening the soil. After digging for about ten inches, I found a letter enwrapped in linoleum:

Блядь! I am not angry with you. When I couldn't find you or your clothes in the room, I didn't even bother searching. I just think I can understand you better now. Come. Or don't! The choice is yours. Dawn in Moscow is best felt in Gorky Park.

Evdokiya

This had played a seriously surprising role. After reading it twice, I made it a single fold and felt the existence of the letter by wandering it around my fingers, as if doubting it being real. I was ashamed of myself for what I had said to God, I put the talisman that pointed at my running away into my pocket and returned home to pack my things.

* * *

When I got home the door was half open. As I got inside, I saw Mete Aga sitting in the living room, aware of nothing.

"Oh, Attila! Sorry, I just came for some domashna rakia. Then I decided to wait for you and drink it here, not to behave shamefully", said Mete Aga, as he stopped the glass at halfway on its way to his mouth. He was playing Old Russian songs on the cassette player he had brought with him.

I sat next to him and filled the glass he had kept empty

for me and hitting his glass, which he had emptied at the same time I had filled mine, I said:

"Cheers, Mete Aga!" I said and after taking a small sip from the glass, I added "By the way, I'm leaving soon".

"You're going? Where are you going again?" he asked.

"I'll go to Moscow the day after next. Apparently journey time has arrived again."

"Moscow? Did the Ruskinyas convince you? Hahaha! Joking aside, you practically just came back from a journey. What journey is this?"

"It's the function, not the duration, Mete Aga.

"What happened this time, Attila?"

"Nothing happened, or maybe a revolution… I'll see when I get there", I said and ended the topic, raising my full glass "C'mon, cheers!"

Even if he didn't let on that much, Mete Aga had gotten a hold of the issue. Without raking it up any further, he began telling about the memories of old times, in line with my questions.

After listening to what he said for more than an hour, I let him go so that he could rise before dawn and successfully start his new drinking session. Before going out the door, Mete Aga turned around and said "Hey Attila, bring some paper and a pen." and after fiddling inside his valet for a while, he took out a phone number.

After adding "Look, this is the number of the son of a very old friend of mine whom I met in Ukraine. He's been in Moscow for quite a long time. If you need anything there, make sure to call him. He'll help you in any way", he wrote the number and left.

Now it was my time to get ready too. Taking advantage

of the internet of the technology world, I bought a one-way ticket from Sofia to Moscow for the next day and brought down my empty suitcase waiting on top of the wardrobe to be filled. Even though we were only at the end of June, I was sure winter would reach Moscow long before Bulgaria so I put my black coat in first.

* * *

The trip is tomorrow at noon and this was my last day in Plovdiv. It had taken my whole night to prepare the suitcase. Actually it was just a 20 minute job, but because I gave a drinking break after every piece I put in, it had spread into quite a long period of time.

As soon as I sobered up, I went to Apartment 101 to say goodbye to Plovdiv. The last bottle of bourbon in Plovdiv!

Although it wasn't dark yet, as usual it was dim inside Apartment 101 as if it were the night, and the man with the hat had taken my place. At least today it could have been vacant. Knowing that the result wouldn't change much, I headed to the bar and sat on a stool.

The new barman replied his own question without even asking it "Yes, I'm giving you double bourbon same as always".

"One bottle of the same", I added.

"Yes alright, I'll pour from the same bottle."

"No, put a full one of the same bottle."

"You want me to open a new bottle and serve from that?" he asked with the surprise of not fully understanding.

"No, put a full bottle of the same in front of me. Of course with a glass and some ice together with it would be fine."

After he submitted his petition saying "Sorry, I misunderstood. It is the first time somebody gets a bottle on his own", he took a new bottle from under the bar with a smile and put it in front of me along with a glass and a small bucket full of ice. Even though he was a seasoned bartender, he hadn't faced this situation before. I wasn't accustomed to it myself either, but I was also passing through a period I wasn't accustomed to. Yesterday was spoiled. Tomorrow is inside a deep unknown.

I emptied the first glass I filled with one sip, took a small sip as soon as I filled the second one and went out to the balcony for a smoke.

When I got onto the balcony the park that filled the city was in front of me again and the post office right next to it. Although it was still about to get dark, the park's lights were lit. The lighting seemed very weak, just like a flag at half-mast.

Taking pleasure in reducing my paranoia to reality, perhaps Plovdiv was mourning for my departure. Now, right now, a graffiti that I had seen before appeared in front of my eyes again: You being paranoid doesn't mean they are not following you.

At this moment, it is inevitable for me to grant this writing right, with its personal effects. Tomorrow, I am leaving Plovdiv after staying for a very short while and it had half-masted its flag for the sake of this mourning, as it saw whips heavier than the price of my sins gnawing my soul. In the meantime, darkness had set in quietly and revealed the moon.

The moon would rise again in Plovdiv but I will not see the tone of its blueness. But I cannot stay. Not that I can't stay, but I won't stay any longer. Staying will pose sorrow as it always does.

As I went back to my place at the bar and refilled from the bottle the glass I had emptied again, the brunette sitting at my right said "A good choice, bourbon", with her good humour, wandering her finger over the empty glass in front of her.

As I filled my own glass and then filled hers too, extending the bottle, I said "I can only share this fine drink with you", without taking my eyes off the drink I poured slowly.

"You talk different. Are you a foreigner?" she asked and took a sincere sip from her glass I had filled.

"Maybe."

"Where are you from?"

"Some place on earth."

Without breaking the smile that suited her cheeks, keeping her silence, she took a few sips from her drink. I had finished my glass and moved to the next one. After a while, she couldn't wait and asked her question again:

"Have you been in Plovdiv long?"

"A month. And a life…"

"Interesting. What do you do here anyway? Most people don't appraise a long time for this place. In fact, recently everyone is trying to run from Bulgaria to Europe."

"That's their problem. I am not them, lady. I had come

here to find peace again, just like the one I had here long ago. But, I was wrong this time."

When she asked "So you'll leave?" I extended my glass and hit hers, without looking at her face, and said "To the last night in Plovdiv!" then finished my glass in a single sip and filled the next one. Abiding by my drinking speed, the alcohol had begun showing its effects.

"Hmm… Where are you going?"

"To some place on earth."

"So you're going back to where you came from? Or to another place where you'll appraise a life to?"

"The single life one possesses can be gifted to only one place."

"I see."

"Good."

"So, will you come back to Plovdiv?"

I turned my face to her and after presenting my looks, which only I could understand, I emptied my again halved glass in a single go, and as I filled a new one, I saw her empty glass and filled that too. Afterwards, I placed the bottle in front of me symmetrically and caressing the bottle's label, I said:

"Like I said, I can only share this fine booze with you. If you'll excuse me, miss. I have something to get over with" and went out onto Apartment 101's balcony, taking a cigarette from the box of Davidoffs in my pocket.

I thought of all the lost ramblers suddenly. I had mental pictures of each of them one by one. We were strong. We were invincible. We were the brazen hearted but we were lost all the same. We had forgotten the path we belonged to while trying to dress the wounds of the past; gotten lost while running from the obscurity of the future. We were ramblers but, hey, we were good people! We were people who made not a slightest compromise from our honour, challenging impossibility for our loved ones. Only, the fact that we were too tired to look for the path we had lost, made us look bad.

Plovdiv was still the same but the rules of the game in this gamble of life had changed now. The memories of this city would be all that were left from all the lost ones. The park's lights were even weaker. When I leaned from the balcony and looked to my right, I saw that the lighting of the statue on top of Aliosha Hill was completely turned off. Probably because of the municipality's weekday savings. I'm not aware of the results of the recent election but, among the candidates, I hope the mature blonde woman I saw frequently on propaganda banners has won. I guess she won't make any difference but I think she suits Plovdiv more than the other shafts. Who wouldn't want to see a dame, who can pour the colour of her eyes into sincerity, as mayor?

When I got back I saw the chick with a sweet smile had gone and that my bottle had reached to a quarter-full. When I picked up my glass, I saw a small sorry-ass fly that had fallen into it. "Fuck it, Attila!" I grumbled to myself. I longly quaffed the remaining quarter bottle. Plovdiv will always be here and its soul will never change, just like the human eye that can remain the same from childhood till under the ground.

"Hey bartender!" I said "I have a question for you".

"Yes, I'm listening."

I turned around and looked at the guy with a hat, who

almost always took my place, and asked "Do you know who that guy in the corner is?"

"Him? He is the person to whom people with stories worth listening to must go", he said and took the glass I was not using from in front of me and left. After trying to scrape the bottom of the bottle some more, I went to the place-taker hatted guy.

"Can you make forbidden words perform a strip-tease?" I asked.

"Tell me", he said.

I sat in the chair across him and signalled the bartender to bring a new bottle. After coughing a bit and clearing my throat, I started my words:

"Once upon a time…"

Printed in Great Britain
by Amazon